# DEADER THAN DEAD

## J.M. GRIFFIN

ISBN: 978-1-7325174-9-3

I0640502

## DEDICATION

I strive for different settings in the State of Rhode Island as interesting backdrops for Vinnie Esposito's adventures. This time around, I selected Block Island, Rhode Island for just that purpose. The island is a marvelous place, with stunning views, kind people, and incredible food and hospitality.

When I first mentioned the idea of using Block Island to Jean Cipriano, a super and longtime friend of mine with enough enthusiasm for ten people, she dug into her memorabilia saved from the years she dwelled on the island as a youngster. She shared stories of various locations that I found of interest, and when I took the ferry to Block Island, I wasn't disappointed. The places she recommended fit the bill more times than not.

Thanks Jean, for your enthusiasm, patience, and best of all for those tall tales that piqued my imagination.

# ACKNOWLEDGMENTS

The Providence Police Department and the Rhode Island State Police have been instrumental in helping to keep my procedures accurate. Thanks all!

# Chapter 1

Before a dead man bobbed against my feet, I was dangling them over the edge of the pier in the inlet's salty marsh water, sunrise on Block Island had been my favorite time of day. I usually drank my coffee and mused while watching the sun peek over the horizon. The warm glow would slowly appear as constant cool breezes off the Atlantic Ocean ruffled my long curls, and the sun would fill my energy reservoir.

I shiver when I think of the deceased man's white skin, bleached by the water and the lack of blood circulation. The memory of his eyes, filmed over with milky-looking mucous, along with missing chunks of flesh on his face, still gave me the willies.

As I recall, I hadn't moved that quickly in a long time. Not until Dembrotti made his untimely entrance into my life, that is. Of course, at the time I had no idea he was Emilio Dembrotti, a thug, hustler, and illegal gaming specialist, among other things. It also wouldn't have made any difference if I'd tried to save him at that juncture, because when you're as disgustingly dead as he was . . . you're dead. There were no two ways about it, the man was deader than dead.

The local *LEO*, law enforcement officer, later delivered the tidbit of news regarding the man's identification. I hadn't recognized Emilio, but then, he didn't look like the dapper man I'd been mildly acquainted with. To make matters worse, the cop insisted on annoying the snot out of me when he had asked repetitious questions, in a variety of ways, with a snarky attitude. He had received the same answers over and over in one way, snappy. Our conversation slipped through my mind.

"You're telling me you didn't know the victim was Emilio Dembrotti?" Officer Martin asked for the umpteenth time.

I took a deep breath, started to count to ten, got as far as four, and stood up. "Am I speaking a foreign language?"

I stepped toward the lanky man with an Adams apple the size of a golf ball. It bobbed up and down the same way Dembrottis body had in the water. I have to admit, David Martin held his ground. I guess that a tall woman of five-foot-ten didn't faze him in the least, though his brown eyes had grown a tad wider when I took a step closer.

"There's no reason to get angry, Ms. Esposito. I have to ask these questions. It's my job."

"Really? You have to ask the same questions over and over in as many different ways as possible?" I snorted and continued, "Just so you know, I'm not stupid, I teach criminal justice. I realize you have a job to do, but you're getting on my last, and tiniest, nerve."

By now my voice had climbed a few octaves and my hand had sneaked to my hip. Both were distinct signs of aggravation, indicating that my Italian attitude had kicked in. The only other telltale sign would have been if I had flipped my hair off my shoulders. Since my mass of unruly brunette curls were gathered in a hair clip, that hadn't happened. The memory of that episode ebbed like the tide, and I heaved a sigh.

My name is Lavinia 'Vinnie' Esposito. Unfortunately for me, these particular circumstances are all too common in my life. Dead people, mobsters, the FBI, and such, aren't foreign to me in the least. Much to my parents, Gino and Theresa Esposito's, chagrin, I often find myself involved in scary situations that tend to be way too dangerous for those who live in a mundane world.

When I'm not teaching cops to be cops at a local Rhode Island university, I hang out at the deli near my house. My best friend, Lola Trapezi, owns the Salt & Pepper Deli in the historic town of Scituate, Rhode Island. The village is small, the town widespread, and for the most part, it's a well-heeled community.

Lola's a woman with common sense, or so my father says, and lives not far from me. My two-family home in Scituate is listed on the historic register and nestles among others of its kind in the peaceful village. I reside in the first floor apartment of the humongous building, and an undercover, absolutely scrumptious FBI agent, Aaron Grant, rents the second floor. Unbeknownst to most, I strive for a mundane life. So far, it hasn't happened.

With warm brown eyes, a year-round tan, and a brilliant smile that charms nearly everyone he meets, Aaron is secretive, caring, and he has saved my butt more often than I can count. He also hangs out at the top of my wish list now that my former beau, Marcus Richmond, and I have gone our separate ways. Wary of inviting his attentions after having called it a day with Marcus, I linger on the fringe of romance with Aaron. I do admit, though, that I have reservations over the fact that Aaron is an undercover FBI agent who wonders if my father is somehow associated with the mob. Frankly, I often wonder the same thing, though I keep my own counsel on that particular subject.

Getting back to the dead man . . . I'd fumbled in my pocket for my cell phone and called the police after losing my balance and nearly falling off the pier. I'd jumped up and scrambled to stay upright when I saw what had bobbed against my feet. Just what I needed was to float around in the water with a dead man. Yikes!

Listening to the call go through, I kept watch over the floater. Thankfully, the salt marsh was an inlet and the pier wasn't on the ocean itself. Otherwise, the surf might have taken him back as fast as he'd been delivered.

Once I'd spoken to the dispatcher at the police station, I realized the cops would soon show up. Block Island is a small, unique island of interwoven connecting roads. The small police department wasn't that far from here. Unwilling to leave the dead body, I waited until I heard a vehicle arrive. A car door closed with a thud that echoed in the peaceful calm of the morning. I peeked over the edge of the pier before I strode forward to meet the officer.

We met at the walkway where a stone path left off and thick, wooden planks extended over the water. His walk was filled with purpose, while his face held a no-nonsense expression.

He dipped his hat-covered head and introduced himself as Officer Dave Martin. His cool, brown-eyed, glance flicked over my shoulder as he spoke, and he grimaced when I explained my find. Great, a cranky-pants cop. Well, damn!

"You made the call?"

"Yes. The body is over there." I pointed to the end of the pier and accompanied by Martin, I moved forward.

He peered into the water, took a long look before he straightened, then gave me another once over and glanced at the house.

"Is Mrs. Trapezi, or anyone else, in residence with you?" Martin asked.

"There are three of us, Lola, Mrs. Trapezi, and me. I believe Lola and her Nana are still asleep."

Martin peered at me and asked, "Why didn't you wake them?"

I tucked wind-driven wisps of hair behind my ears and said, "I didn't want to leave the body."

He nodded and spoke into the microphone attached to his shoulder strap, ordered an ambulance and a body bag and then waited. The answer to his request wasn't clear, but I figured we'd soon have company. Geez, I hated being the bearer of bad news.

"He looks like he's snagged there, he's not going anywhere. We might as well wake everyone. While we're at it, you can answer some questions for me." He grasped my arm. I gave him a look, the kind your mother gave you as a kid when you'd been bad. He dropped his hand and motioned me along the walk.

That's when things got out of control. I entered the house one step ahead of him to find Lola standing in the kitchen, staring out the window. She turned her gaze toward me, rolled her eyes, and shook her head.

"Don't even tell me there's a dead person out there?" Lola demanded while she stared at me, her dark brown eyes filled with disbelief.

"You guessed it. That's exactly what's out there," I murmured. I placed my coffee cup on the counter in hope she'd fill it to the brim with an added shot of whiskey.

"You're not throwing up, so it's safe to say there wasn't any blood involved." Lola peered past me. She gave Martin a look and asked if he wanted a cup of coffee.

Lola Trapezi owns a head of wild, curly, rich auburn hair, a face full of freckles, and has a Julia Roberts smile that knocks men off their feet. They get stupid and foolish when she offers up the Julia smile, but this time around the smile was absent. She'd been going through a rough patch lately and had little humor to spare. Like Elvis, Lola's usual charm had left the building, so to speak.

Officer Martin mumbled that he'd be grateful for coffee and left it at that. His glance flicked around the solid cottage with its weather worn shingles and six-over-six pane windows. The floors, a bit crooked from age, and the house were in good shape from having been cared for over the years.

"You must be vacationing," Martin stated.

"We're just here for a few weeks," Lola answered as she handed each of us cups of fresh coffee with no whiskey involved.

I slid a glance in her direction. She planned to stay more than a week? When had that decision been made? Reluctant to ask while Martin was present, I kept my mouth shut.

By this time, the rescue had arrived. Martin told us to stay put until he returned. Where had he thought we would go? After all, we were on a small island in the Atlantic Ocean, off the coast of Rhode Island, and without a boat handy.

He joined the medical crew, directed them to the body and instructed them on its removal. The windows were wide open. I listened to him, well aware that I had no bargaining chips on this island. This wasn't Providence, and I hadn't taught criminal justice to these people. Nobody on Block Island owed me any favors, which meant if things got complicated I was on my own. Crap.

While the crew went about their business, Lola stood silent and listened to Martin's instructions, just as I had. When I turned to look at her, she shook her head and murmured, "You're at a disadvantage this time, Vin."

With a brief nod, I said, "I know."

Martin rejoined Lola and me as footsteps tapped down the stairs. Lola's grandmother, Nana, was up and about. I took a deep breath before I met her in the doorway.

"What's going on here? Is that a policeman?" Nana demanded as she watched Martin hike the steps to the screen door.

I put an arm around her shoulder. "Nana, there's been an accident. A man drowned. I found him in the marsh while watching the sun rise this morning. I had to call the police, you understand, don't you?"

She nodded. "Dave Martin, is that you?" Nana squinted up at his six-foot frame from her pert four-and-a-half foot height.

"Mrs. Trapezi, I'm sorry to bother you first thing this morning," Martin apologized quickly. "I have some questions for Ms. Esposito."

"Well, get on with it then. I'm going back to bed for a bit," Nana remarked and turned on her heel. With a wink at Lola and me, Nana shuffled up the stairs in her squat-heeled, dainty slippers, adorned with fluffy feathers atop the pink satin.

Stifling a chuckle, I turned to Martin and plunked into the nearest chair. His questions began again. I answered them. He kept asking, and I kept answering, the same questions over and over. This went on for some time until I lost patience and offered him a narrow-eyed glare.

Martin's lips pressed tight. He glanced from Lola, to me, and then back again. His radio crackled, and he seemed to come to a decision.

"I have to return to headquarters. I'll let you know when I have information, and by the way, there's bound to be more questions. Remain on the island."

We nodded as he left. Lola glanced at me from her seat at the table and let out a sigh of relief.

"Vin, who was the dead guy?"

"How would I know? I'm not from Block Island. He was disgusting to look at, so I might not have recognized him if I did know him."

"Let's hope he isn't a mobster. Let's also hope he simply got drunk and fell overboard from his yacht or something," Lola said on a weary note.

I refrained from telling her about the rope around his neck. Lola said she'd get dressed while I made breakfast. I nodded and set about the task.

# Chapter 2

"I'm heading to the store, Nana needs groceries," Lola called up the stairs.

My shorts zipped and shirt straightened, I glanced in the mirror and said I'd be right with her.

Skipping down the narrow staircase, I joined Lola at the door. Our time on the island was supposed to be a stress-reliever for Lola, a much needed one. I took in her expression and realized that I'd added to her anxiety by finding the dead man. Not that I wanted to find him, but things of that sort are inevitable in my life. Or so it seems.

I reached out and touched her arm as we walked toward the car.

"I'm really sorry about the dead man bobbing into our lives this morning. Truly, I am."

Lola slid into the front seat of her Mini Cooper. She turned to look at me when I took the passenger seat.

She'd smirked at the *bobbing* remark. "Vin, there's nothing you could have done about that. I might have found him instead, which goes beyond my realm of acceptance. You're used to this sort of thing, while I, on the other hand, cook and bake. Don't worry about me, just look out for yourself. You don't have any allies in this police department and that won't bode well for you."

I swallowed hard. My friendships within police departments on the mainland hadn't turned life problematic when I ended up in a tight spot. It wouldn't be so easy this time. An uncomfortable sensation squirreled down my spine at what possibilities might lie ahead. I wondered if it was fear.

"It isn't as if *I* killed him."

"How do you know he was killed?" Lola wanted to know.

Unwilling to say, I just shrugged.

We stopped at the intersection and Lola glanced at me. She held the steering wheel in a white-knuckled grip.

"Just freakin' tell me, Vin," she snapped.

"He kind of had a rope around his neck?" I said in a question-like tone.

"Christ, why didn't you tell me that before?" Her voice hiked another notch.

"You're having a rough go of things right now. I didn't want to burden you."

Lola gaped at me, went through the stop sign, and asked, "Didn't you think that tidbit of news would eventually come out?"

"I guess." I glanced out of the car window. We were at the market.

"Let's get this over with and return to the house, I need to cook. It's my salvation," Lola remarked.

With a nod, I walked alongside her into the store. She raced up and down the aisles as though chased by the devil. Her petite stature didn't matter; the woman was on a mission. Even though I'm long legged, she moved as fast as lightening, and I lengthened my stride to keep up.

"Go two aisles over and pick up a five-pound bag of flour. I'll meet you at the check-out counter," Lola ordered.

"Will do." I swerved away from her.

I'd rounded the end-cap of the aisle and ran smack into Dave Martin. Lucky me.

"Excuse me, ma'am." Martin said and grasped my arm as I bounced off him and upended his hand basket of goods. His tall, lanky body was the same height as mine, which was just two inches short of six feet tall. He had a wiry kind of strength. His brown eyes matched his hair color and though he wasn't strikingly handsome, he wasn't ugly either, though the oversized Adam's apple was a tad disconcerting.

"Oh, sorry," I answered and looked at him in surprise. I knelt, helping him retrieve the food that rolled willy-nilly across the floor.

"I was going to call you shortly. You need to come to headquarters," Martin said in a soft voice as he glanced at people who'd stopped to stare at our collision.

"Oh, uh, okay. I have return to the house with Lola, and then I'll head over."

Martin nodded, gave me directions, and I left him staring after me. I scooped the bag of flour from the shelf before joining Lola at the check-out counter.

"You look upset. What's up?" Lola asked as I stepped into the line.

Giving her a *not now* nod, I murmured, "I'll tell you later."

After the groceries were bagged and stowed in the car, we headed to Nana's. I explained what had happened and asked to use the car.

Lola handed over the keys and advised, "You might consider getting a lawyer, Vin."

"Aren't you getting ahead of yourself? Why do I need a lawyer? I didn't kill the guy, it's apparent he'd been dead quite some time. I was just unfortunate enough to find him, is all."

"At least call Aaron or Marcus," Lola suggested softly as she swung the car into the driveway.

I considered her advice while taking the groceries into the kitchen. That's when my inner voice kicked in. *You'll feel better if you call them. They can help you. They won't judge you. You need backup.* Yeah, right. As if that idea helped me at all. I shook my head, mentally groused about a shut off switch for my internal voice and frowned over what lay ahead. If I called anyone, it would be Aaron, especially since Marcus would be unlikely to come near the situation. I was reluctant to involve either man.

Keys in hand, I left Lola to unpack the groceries while she discussed the upcoming meal menu with Nana. Lola glanced up and wished me luck as I opened the screen door.

I smiled, stifling the uncomfortable fear that threatened to engulf me. As innocent as I was, I knew the situation could run out of control. I'd been down that road way too often to not know the realities of finding a dead body. As far as fear went, it's a fairly new feeling for me, one that I'd rarely considered until I'd recently been temporarily kidnapped in another unfortunate scenario.

Parked beside a police cruiser, I locked the Cooper and took in my surroundings. Tourists were everywhere, riding bicycles, motorcycles, scooters, or walking while they absorbed the loveliness of the island. Block Island holds great beauty, it's always breezy, and the day was sunny. The only one with a black cloud hanging overhead was me.

I reached for the station's door handle when the door opened and Officer Martin beckoned me inside. Mindful, I entered his domain.

He gestured to a padded chair next to his desk. "Have a seat over here, Ms. Esposito."

I wondered what his process was for questioning persons of interest at the island's station, compared to the way it was handled on the mainland where you'd be put in a box for questioning. Over there, questioning took place in *the box*, a small, bulletproof glass enclosed room. Glass walls meant other detectives could keep their eye on what was happening, but not get shot if somebody got hold of a gun. That had taken place several years back, resulting in a policeman's death, a hard lesson learned by all.

"We've identified the body," Martin said.

"And he was?" I asked with interest.

"Emilio Dembrotti, a racketeer. Did you know him, Ms. Esposito?"

"No," I answered. *But you did know him in passing* my internal voice reminded me. Where was the shut-off switch?

"Are you sure you didn't know him? Being Italian and all, I thought you might have met," Martin goaded.

"Not all Italians know one another, Officer Martin," I remarked dryly.

"True, true." Martin raised his brows and continued. "So you're telling me you didn't recognize, or know the man?"

I studied my fingernails before I looked up and asked, "Are you deaf?"

"Just doing my job," he answered patiently.

I sat motionless, unwilling to squirm in my seat, lest he think I was a liar. About lying, I admit that I lie by omission, and I cross my fingers and toes while doing so. Sometimes I get away with it, other times I don't. It depends on who's asking the questions and what information I might hold back. Marcus, a Rhode Island State Trooper, has never had Aaron's ability of knowing, down pat, though he'd given it his all.

"We figure he was in the water for a day or so. He'd been strangled with the rope tied around his neck and then was tossed off a boat. The current brought him to the island and the tide sent him into the marsh."

"And?" I asked.

"I just wanted you to know how he arrived at Mrs. Trapezi's pier."

"Well, I'll be sure to tell her," I said in a soft tone while feeling the worst was yet to come.

Tapping a pencil, Martin pulled his attention away from the report in front of him to stare straight at me. "Is it true that you're involved with murder and mayhem on the mainland?"

With a deep breath, I said, "I wouldn't say that exactly. I've had a few issues, but nothing like this."

"Uh, huh." He flicked a file page over and scanned the sheet before bringing his gaze back to me. "It seems you've dealt with, and know, quite a few mobsters, and have helped the police incarcerate some of them. Is that true?"

"I hardly know mobsters. I have assisted the police whenever asked, though."

With an abrupt movement, he slapped the file closed and leaned forward.

"We don't want your help over here, Ms. Esposito. We want you to mind your own affairs and leave the police work to those who are official officers."

Taken aback by his vehemence, I blustered, "Cripes, I only found the body. I'm on vacation, not involved in an investigation. Rest assured that I won't interfere with your work." I rose from the chair and slung my handbag strap onto my shoulder.

"For your own sake, keep it that way," Martin warned with eyes as cold as his features. "And Ms. Esposito, if I find out you've lied to me, it won't go easy for you. Remember, this isn't Providence."

# Chapter 3

When I returned to Nana's house, a motorcycle sat parked in the yard. Apparently Nana had company.

I stepped into the kitchen. Marcus Richmond sat at the table with a tall glass of iced tea and seemed to have schmoozed Nana Trapezi with his trooper charm. He glanced up when I came to a sudden stop inside the doorway.

"Hey, Vin," he said with a smile, though the warmth never reached his eyes.

It was apparent that he'd heard of the deader-than-dead man incident and had taken the quickest means necessary to get here. Since there was a motorcycle in the yard, it was safe to say he'd taken the fast ferry. Why was he here, anyway? Was my life about to hit the crapper, or what?

With a wide, friendly grin, I said, "Hi Marcus, what are you doing here?"

"As of today, I'm assigned to the island for the summer and heard you were here. I thought I'd stop by to see you and Lola."

He knew about Dembrotti, I could tell.

"Great. Where's Lola?" I asked Nana.

"She's lounging on the pier. Dinner is set to go into the oven, and she needs some rest. Do you know what's bothering her?"

Innocently, I asked, "She didn't tell you?"

Nana peered out the window at Lola and remarked, "She hasn't said a word. My granddaughter is looking a bit frayed around the edges. I want to know why, and you're going tell me, right now."

I glanced at Marcus, who leaned back in his chair. A tiny smirk played around his lips as he toyed with his glass. It was plain as day he wouldn't interfere.

"Her parents are getting a divorce, and Lola's upset over it," I confessed.

"Who's divorcing whom? When did this happen?" Nana demanded.

"Two weeks ago, Mr. Trapezi told his wife he wanted a divorce. Bobby feels the way Lola does about the whole thing, but Lola is unraveled by their decision to split up." I sank into the nearest chair and wiped sweat from my brow. I disliked being questioned by a woman who could instill fear in the hearts of men and women alike. To lie, and say I didn't know, would have been foolhardy. Lola and I had been friends for years, and Nana knew I would be fully aware of what had brought her granddaughter to the island.

"Is my son having an affair?" Nana asked with a narrowed gaze.

"I don't know, Lola hasn't said. She's just distressed. When she asked that I come to Block Island with her, I figured it would be good for her to get away and have me along, so I agreed. Nana, I'm sorry about the dead guy."

A snort issued from Marcus. He held his tongue, even though it must have cost him dearly. I glanced at him, offered a nasty glare, and returned my attention to Nana.

She gave me a nod, and went out the back door toward the pier. I turned to Marcus.

"I think it's time we took a walk, Marcus. The two of them don't need an audience, and I've had enough drama today to last me a while."

Marcus got up and nudged me toward the front door.

We ambled along the narrow road for a half-mile or so in silence. Traffic was next to nil, birds chirped, and the breeze smelled of salt and wildflowers. Block Island was an idyllic vacation spot, when there weren't any dead men floating around, that is.

"Lola must be beside herself. I know how close she is to her family," Marcus remarked.

"Her anxiety has hit an all-time high. She can't seem to wrap her head around the fact that her parents will divorce after all these years."

"Do you know why? Really?" Marcus stopped and turned to look at me.

"No, I truly don't, Lola hasn't shared that with me. I'm afraid to ask. When my mother had threatened to leave my father over Tony Jabroni, I was beside myself. I can't imagine why Lola's father wants a divorce. Maybe he's going through a mid-life crisis."

Marcus stared at me for a long time before he nodded. I guessed he accepted the fact that I hadn't lied. "I'm sure Lola appreciates your support, Vin.

"I had to be here for her," I murmured. "She's been there for me at every turn since we were kids. It's awful to see her so depressed." I studied his rock hard features and asked, "You've really been stationed on the island for the summer?"

"Sure have. The guy who was supposed to be here was injured in an accident, and I was ordered to replace him. Why?"

With a shrug, I said, "I thought, uh, never mind."

The island police force is a small one, too small to handle the amount of hair-raising antics that take place as party-goers arrive in their boats, cabin cruisers, sailboats, and what not. Beachside bars provide alcohol and music, and the boats moor so close to one another, it's possible to step from one to the next, and join each party in turn. A Rhode Island State Trooper or two are sent to the island to help keep the peace.

Marcus asked, "You thought I was investigating Emilio Dembrotti, didn't you?"

"Well, yeah, I guess so."

A small sign on our left pitched awkwardly toward the ground and indicated a labyrinth could be found up over the hill. Rickety steps, bordered by a frail handrail, leaned against an embankment. I suggested we take a look.

Marcus held the handrail steady while I lightly treaded the steps to the grounds above us. In an instant, he had joined me.

We meandered through the labyrinth, each of us lost in our own thoughts. I thanked the universe for the many small favors in my life before I asked for guidance where Emilio Dembrotti was concerned. It seemed I would need all the help I could get if the situation with the police department should take a turn for the worse.

I was uncertain of what would happen if Martin found out I knew Dembrotti. Ours had been a brief meeting, one that had attachments to my father. I didn't like the way this could play out, but I'd protect myself and my family at all cost.

Our sojourn through the labyrinth finished, Marcus and I sat on the metal-framed wooden bench perched under overhanging honeysuckle bushes at the top of the slope. The sun was hot and I was sweaty, yet peace and tranquility filled this spot so many others had traversed. I turned to Marcus who stared out over the grounds.

"Why did you really come to the house?"

"I got a call from Trooper Maddox, who's been dispatched here with me. He heard about Dembrotti, that you found him, and figured something bad was about to hit the fan. He decided I should know." Marcus looked at me and asked softly, "You didn't know it was Dembrotti?"

I had been asked this question way too many times today and sighed before answering him.

"No, I didn't. I also wouldn't have recognized him if I'd known him in the first place. He was pretty nasty looking, scavenged by fish, and bobbed around alongside the pier. Why do you ask?"

Marcus sat back and sighed. "I simply wondered if you had known this man or if there was a possible connection to your family."

Dirt clogged my sandals. I tapped them clean and said, "Never knew him, and I don't think my family is familiar with him, either. I know for certain my aunt has never, ever dated him. Satisfied?"

With a shake of his head and a keen stare, he said, "That about covers it, Vin. I hope you're not fibbing to me."

"I have no reason to lie." Though I had, I said it was time to go.

Marcus kissed my cheek, looked off in the distance, and then walked off. I lingered to collect my thoughts as he disappeared over the embankment onto the rickety stairs. I'd begun to stroll downhill, toward the rickety ladder when a sudden movement on my left caught my eye.

When I looked, a wavering image caused me to break out in a sweat. Emilio Dembrotti stood twenty or so feet away in a mirage sort of way. He beckoned me, his eyes bulging and his hands waving. I choked at the sight, glanced away, and then back to Dembrotti, only he was no longer there. Scared senseless, I ran toward the handrail, jumped over the embankment and caught up with Marcus.

He gave me a sideways look, asked if I was all right, and seemed pensive when I nodded. Our return trip to Nana's was silent.

We arrived as a vehicle stopped in front of Nana's house. Elated when Aaron Grant shut off the motor of his Yukon SUV and got out to greet us, we approached him as he waited alongside the truck. My heart began to pound. I wondered if he, too, thought I needed saving, and why.

He and Marcus gave each other a cool nod. I stood aside watching the two macho, A-type, personalities at work. Each man summed up the other in a heartbeat, but remained friendly. Marcus is my main man, he was no longer. Even though I was cautious when it came to giving my heart back to him after all of our recent problems, I trusted him, like no other.

Handsome and understanding were two words I often used to describe Aaron. Manipulating sneaked in there, too, but it was a part of his job and his FBI persona. Marcus was more or less the same, but the manipulating part wasn't as refined. Most of the time, Marcus would come out and ask what he wanted to know. Aaron wasn't above setting a trap in search of answers, should he think I'd lie.

Aaron greeted me, then took in our surroundings before he asked, "Where's Lola?"

I smirked, but answered the question with one of my own.

"Don't tell me, you came all this way to see Lola?" I knew better than that.

"I heard about Dembrotti, and I also knew you were here with Lola. Are you both all right?"

I nodded and murmured, "Lola could use friends right now. Her parents are divorcing and she's not handling it well. Since you've both been in that position with your own parents, maybe you can talk to her about it. I haven't that sort of experience. She's not sharing much and should do so before anxiety eats her alive."

This was a ploy, but not an unfair one. These two men adored Lola. I also needed to get them off my case about Dembrotti. I noticed a glance slide between them and watched as Marcus headed toward the pier. I was now alone to answer more questions from Aaron. *Geesh.*

"Dembrotti was murdered, huh?" Aaron asked.

I answered with, "A rope around his neck did the trick."

"Only you would end up finding this guy. He was a vicious criminal, Vin."

"So I'm told. Officer Martin is a miserable twit, and spent his morning aggravating me. Then he topped that off with a threat that I had nobody on the island to protect me if he found out I'd lied. He acts as if I tied the rope around Dembrotti's neck and tossed him overboard."

The corners of Aaron's mouth tilted upward a bit before he asked, "Martin got to you, didn't he?"

"He really ticked me off. Honestly, I can't get away from the mob, no matter where I go. Of all the places Dembrotti could have turned up, he had to end up here." I rubbed my temples and sighed. The memory of Dembrotti's ghostly image I'd seen at the labyrinth, lay firmly planted in my mind. I shook my head and took a deep breath.

Aaron draped an arm around my shoulders as we strolled past the far side of the house and across the lawn. Several Adirondack chairs were clustered in a circle with a fire pit in the center. We lounged in two of the chairs, both of us stretching our long legs out. While I'm tall, Aaron stands well over six feet. He's well-built and reminds me of Dwayne Johnson, formerly known as The Rock, a famous WWE wrestler turned actor. Brown-eyed with dark hair, Aaron's smile stops you dead and makes your heart race faster than it should. Like I said, he's wish-list material.

"Tell me what happened. All of it, Vin," he asked in a soft voice.

In minutes, I had summed up the day. When I fell silent, I glanced at Aaron.

He shook his head and squeezed my hand. "You do have the worst luck."

"I guess."

"Is anyone aware that you met Dembrotti on Federal Hill last fall?" he asked.

"No, not even Marcus. Dembrotti said he was protecting me from the mob. Imagine? The mob protecting me from the mob? How ironic is that?"

Aaron gave me an even look. "Who sent him to protect you?"

I shrugged and answered him, "He wouldn't say. Just told me it was a favor for a friend. He and his two goons gave me a start, I can tell you that. When one of them asked for my car keys, I thought they planned to stuff me into my own trunk."

"You have no idea who sent him to protect you?"

"None. I'm glad that you were aware I'd met him, though. That way, if I had been stuffed in the trunk, you could have rescued me." I grinned at him as he smiled.

"You really don't lie well. I can't imagine why Marcus couldn't always tell when you were."

I'd had enough questions today to sink a ship. My sense of humor evaporated as I turned to him with a snappy response. "Okay, get this, even if I knew who had sent him, it isn't any of your damned business, so back off."

He raised his hands to ward off the razor-sharp retort. "I was only asking. No need to get jumpy."

"Do you know how often I've been questioned today? At the market, in the kitchen, at the police station . . . everywhere. I'm tired of answering stupid questions. I'd like some peace and quiet, but no, not me, no luck here." I was on a roll that was going downhill fast.

"Vin, take it easy, I'm sorry. I should have known you'd be upset over this. Let's talk about something else."

I sighed. "Like what?"

"Lola."

"She needed a vacation, and not just because of her parents," I said. "Honestly, she's falling apart. You should really spend some time with her, Aaron. She needs all the support she can get. I'm not sure what else is bothering her, but something is."

He left the chair and strode away. I watched him disappear around the corner of the house toward the pier where Lola and Marcus idly sat, side-by-side. I wanted nothing more than some quiet time and took off on foot.

# Chapter 4

Half an hour later, I'd reached the main street of the island where restaurants, gift shops and more, awaited tourists. Exercise had brightened my mood, offering a better outlook. I'd told Nana that I was off for a walk and promised to return by dinner time.

I watched as an enormous ferry dropped anchor. Sightseers filled the sidewalks and a single motorbike rental area only had two Mopeds left, the other stands were closed. The skinny vacant lot, where scooters and Mopeds were usually lined up, lay covered in a bed of brown, mashed-down grass. Dust, from parched dirt, swirled about, by the breeze rolling in offshore. The ocean and beach lay across the road.

I stepped up to the girl wearing tight jeans, way too much black eye-liner, and chewing a wad of gum. I asked how much it cost to rent a Moped.

Her hand fluttered like a leaf in the wind as she told me the price and added that I needed to pay cash. I glanced past her. There was no stand for a credit card machine or even a cash register. Her jeans pockets bulged, and tips of twenty-dollar bills filtered past a pocket edge. I wondered why she didn't have a credit card device and thought maybe she couldn't get good cell phone reception here. I stepped close to her.

"Here you go," I said and doled cash into her outstretched hand.

I took the keys and walked the sweet machine onto the street. The motor puttered, then revved, and I took off like a shot with no idea where I was going. I simply needed to be alone and free-wheeling for a while.

The roads on Block Island are more country lanes that wind, twist, and intersect throughout the island. Some roads run along the shoreline while others travel inland, but none are far from the ocean. I took a left onto Cooneymus Road and drove for a while until a sharp curve caught me unaware. The angle of it hadn't given me much time to brake, and as I rounded the bend an apparition lingered in the middle of the road in front of me. Dembrotti hovered, the rope around his neck hanging down the front of his shirt.

Panic grabbed me hard and I swerved, skidded sideways, and in a slow motion-like action, I went in the direction of a low stone wall. The scooter slammed head-on into the stacked stones. As one, the vehicle and I went airborne past the *Rodman's Hollow* signpost and I let go of the scooter's handlebars. Somewhere nearby, I heard the bike hit the ground and tumble again and again. I was too concerned about my own descent to worry much about it.

Hands and arms outstretched, I grabbed for anything that came my way to stay my trip into the forested area below. Within moments, or maybe seconds, I came to a sudden stop, landing against a squishy mass.

Dirt and forest debris covered my body, hair, and clothes. It took a while for my head to stop spinning before I got my bearings. Little did I know what lay underneath me.

A stench rose from the mass, and crab-like, I scrambled sideways to escape the offensive smell. Scrubbing my dirty hands against my jeans, before I swept my jumbled hair back from my face. I then brushed dirt from my eyes and face, then gaped at the ravaged body that had broken my fall.

The dead man had come to rest twenty feet or so from the base of a dense stand of trees that filled the hollow. I was thankful my fall had been broken, but not necessarily by means of a dead body. Two dead guys in the same day? Who'd have thought I could get so lucky?

Unable to take my eyes off the horrid corpse, I peered at the swollen body. Maggots wiggled on his face, squirmed out of his nose and fell from his ear lobes. My stomach roiled. He was fully clothed in vacation attire, and a rope around his neck mingled with the collar of his shirt. My pulse raced as I peered at my surroundings, searching the trees further on for another body or the ghost of Dembrotti. Nothing else was down here that I could see, other than me, the corpse, and my rented, very smashed, Moped. Dang, I hate when this stuff happens.

I reached for my cell phone and found it wasn't in my pocket. I patted my clothes for the small instrument, and realized I'd lost it in my downhill tumble.

I took stock of my limbs before I stood up. A sharp pain radiated from my ankle and spiked up my calf. In my haste to get away from the corpse, I hadn't noticed the pain. I stopped applying pressure to the foot and gingerly plunked onto the ground once again. My arms and remaining body parts seemed fine, the ankle was another matter. The afflicted area had already started to swell over my sandal strap, though no bones protruded from the skin, and thankfully no blood oozed from a wound. If there had been blood, I'd have been tossing my breakfast onto the hillside. I detest blood, and vomit every time I see it. Not a pretty sight, that.

With the hill that rose behind me, I knew it would take some doing since I couldn't walk, which meant crawling my way up was my only option. The moped had seen better days. Even if I could have, I wouldn't consider hauling it up behind me. The body, well, it would rest in place until someone lifted it out, that person would not be me.

The ascent wasn't as bad as I'd imagined as long as I kept my ankle from snagging on roots, rocks, and whatever else protruded from the hillside. Not quite successful at keeping it from hitting this or that, eventually I made it to the stone wall. On the way up I found my phone covered in dirt and grime, but still intact.

I dialed Nana's house. She answered on the second ring. I asked to speak with Marcus and was told he was no longer there. I asked for Aaron and got the same answer. I finally asked for Lola and felt a wave of relief wash over me when she came on the line.

"Where are you?" Lola asked. Concern riddled her voice.

"I'm at Rodman's Hollow. Can you come get me?"

"Rodman's Hollow?" she repeated. "You're at Rodman's Hollow?"

Was I speaking a foreign language today or was everyone freakin' deaf? I took a deep breath and asked again, "Can you come get me? I'll explain when you arrive. Call the police, too, while you're at it."

"Right, you want to report an accident, is that it?"

I couldn't tell from her voice if she was trying to figure out what had happened or if she was simply resigned to my odd requests.

"Sort of. I just need a ride." I ended the call and pocketed the phone. I'd settled on the stone wall with my foot raised to relieve the pain and swelling, and stared at the body below. His clothing blended into the foliage, making it difficult to discern his location unless you knew he was there.

Who was he? Where had he come from? Why was he there? Had his body been dumped? Why did he, like Dembrotti, have a rope around his neck?

It hit me that both men had been killed the same way. I wished I'd searched his clothes for identification and quickly shivered at the thought of searching a corpse, especially one covered with maggots. I checked my clothes for any of those wiggly little darlings and found none. We all need to be thankful for the small things in life.

Lola drew the car to a stop and got out. Her eyes widened as she looked me over. When she saw my ankle, she blanched and gasped at the same time.

"You should have said you were injured, Vin. How did that happen?" Lola pointed at my ankle and waited.

I explained the trip down the hollow, and the body below. As I spoke, she stepped to the wall and leaned over to stare downward. I showed her where the body was. It took her some time, but eventually she saw the dead man.

A siren sounded, and a police car came into view, then stopped behind Lola's car. Martin sat behind the steering wheel. Could my day get any worse?

"You called the police?" he asked Lola while giving me a keen stare.

"Yes, Vinnie's had an accident, and you'd better take a look over the wall there." She jerked her thumb toward the hollow.

"You're one busy woman, Ms. Esposito. First a dead floater and now you've crashed a Moped over the wall."

Apparently he hadn't seen the body.

"Look closer. The Moped is the least of our problems." I remarked and trained his eyes with my index finger to the body below. I heard the sharp intake of his breath as he studied the shadowed landscape.

"That would be a dead man, Officer Martin," I said.

He spoke into the microphone attached to his shoulder strap and requested an ambulance be sent to our location.

Martin turned to me after a muffled response from police headquarters. It always amazed me how officers understood the static replies and orders they received that way. Maybe I was hard of hearing.

Are you seriously injured?" Martin asked with a sign of what I took as compassion.

"Just my ankle. I probably look the worse for wear. Thanks for asking."

Martin nodded and made his way down the slope toward the body. He slid and stumbled his way, but never lost his footing. Why couldn't I have done that? *Could have been because he wasn't flying through the air after seeing a ghost* my inner voice responded. *You're really in the soup now.* I muttered for it to shut up. Lola slanted a questioning glance in my direction. I shook my head and sighed.

The rescue team arrived minutes later. We directed the crew to where Officer Martin stood. He yelled to them to bring the sleigh-basket along with a body bag. Amazed by their efficiency, I watched the team go into action.

A long coffin-shaped basket came into view with a neatly folded black bag tightly secured in the center of it. The basket was used for lifting people from difficult places. I figured Rodman's Hollow fit that bill perfectly.

Lola and I watched the process while awaiting permission to leave for the emergency room. Why Martin hadn't yet allowed us to depart left me wondering if he had an ulterior motive or if he wanted to torture me for a while. My ankle, now balloon-like, pained me terribly. I detested this cop, I really did.

Once the corpse was lifted from the hollow, Martin allowed us to leave with a warning that he'd have questions later on. I nodded, Lola struggled to help me get into the car, and we scooted away. Why no one else stepped forward to assist me was a mystery. Who would want to hang around with a dead guy and his maggots? I was happy to leave the scene.

The car cruised NASCAR-style toward the hospital. I thought we might have been in qualifying mode by the way Lola drove. Her brows furrowed, her bottom lip clenched between her teeth, Lola was in no mood for interference. There'd be no help for anyone who dared to stop us now.

We parked in front of the emergency room doors. Lola told me to stay put, ran through the sliding glass doors as they opened, and disappeared into the building. Within moments, she steered a wheelchair toward the car. I obliged her by sitting in it to be wheeled inside and cared for, and decided I might get some pity here, if nowhere else.

A male nurse deposited me in a cubicle, helped me onto a gurney, released my sandal strap, and then cleaned the afflicted area. He left me alone for a few moments, then returned with the doctor.

The young man, who didn't look old enough to shave, introduced himself as Dr. Fortin. He probed the ankle until I thought I'd jump off the gurney and pummel him into the floor. It was at that point he sent me for an x-ray.

There was no easy way to x-ray the ankle without contributing to my agony, so gritting my teeth, I resigned myself to it. When I was wheeled into the same cubicle after the pictures were taken, Dr. Fortin declared the ankle was sprained, but not broken.

Relieved, I listened to his advice while he wrapped an elastic bandage around and around my foot. Clipped in place, the bandage resembled a huge ball of fabric, except it was on my foot and aggravating me.

I thanked the doctor and staff, allowed Lola to roll me into the lobby, where I gave my medical information to the woman at the desk. Slowly, I hobbled toward the car on a pair of crutches. Have I ever said how I feel about crutches? They're a real pain to use.

# Chapter 5

Fortunately, the drive to Nana's was done at a slower pace than the ride to the emergency room had been. Lola, intent on our arrival in one piece, stated that supper would probably be cold since we'd been gone so long.

Guilt rolled over me while I listened to her. She'd been intense over our issues, and had turned that intensity on dinner, or the lateness of it. I sighed, apologized, and watched as she turned her gaze to me.

"You have nothing to apologize for." Her auburn curls fluttered in the sea breeze as she held the crutches while I exited the car. "It isn't your fault these jerks got killed, and you crashed that Moped. Not your fault, at all."

I gazed after her as she flounced toward the house. Lola was in the middle of a crisis. Her own crisis. We really needed to talk.

Dinner was on the table, wine glasses were filled, and crescent-shaped rolls nestled in a cloth napkin-draped basket beside a luscious chicken casserole. A light repast, nothing heavy, was just what we all needed. Dinner was a quiet affair with nobody feeling the need for small talk. Even my inner voice was silent.

Marcus and Aaron were absent, which gave me cause to wonder why. My clothing had been exchanged for a warmer outfit after I'd managed a shower that included a plastic bag wrapped tightly over my foot wrap. My ankle throbbed, but I refused to give in. I took a couple of over-the-counter pain relievers and hoped for the best. The evening wore on.

I hobbled across the lawn to settle into an Adirondack chair opposite Lola. She sat bundled in a ruffle-edged afghan she'd brought from the house. I swirled a crocheted shawl around my shoulders, wrapping it tight against the never-ending wind that blew in off the Atlantic. There was no respite from it anywhere on the island, except at the bottom of Rodman's Hollow where the forest was dense, the incline steep, and the lowest point was protected from the ocean. A better dumping ground, I couldn't imagine.

"You want to talk about what's on your mind? I'm a real good listener, you know," I said to Lola.

She didn't answer right away, but stared out over the grounds toward the inlet. When I'd about given up hope that Lola would share, she mumbled, "I'm not a Trapezi."

That was when she began to cry. I stared at her, thinking I might not have heard her correctly. The puzzle pieces snapped together as I realized the reason for the divorce between Lola's parents. Speechless, I waited to see if Lola would offer anything other than those four words.

"I know you're bursting at the seams to ask a billion questions, and that you have been since I told you about the divorce in the first place," Lola said as she turned her tear drenched gaze toward me. "I appreciate the space you've given me, but I have to tell someone, and it's got to be you."

I leaned forward a tad and murmured softly, "So, tell me then."

"Years ago, while my father was away for a couple of months on business, my mother had a fling. She got pregnant and passed me off as a Trapezi. The fact that I have red hair and Bobby has the classic Italian looks of my father's family didn't seem to faze anyone. There are redheads on my mother's side of the family tree that go back a hundred years." She plucked at a thread on the rim of the afghan, tucking it into itself so it wouldn't unravel.

Puzzled, I said, "Go on."

"The guy blew out of my mother's life as fast as he'd arrived. He was never heard from again, I guess. At least that's the story Mom has given us all. Bobby is beside himself, but I am just . . . I don't know what I am anymore, or who I am for that matter." She wept a bit more, sniffled, and then sat back with a hiccup.

I reached over and patted her shoulder.

"Lola, you're the same person you've always been. Nothing can take that away from you. Don't wear the blame for your mother's indiscretion like a mantle on your shoulders. Parents do stupid stuff, they're human. When my mother threatened to leave my father, it was horrible, but it was up to them to straighten it out, not Giovanni and me. I know you're sad and confused about this, but it's not your fault." I leaned closer to her. "You're a terrific person, no matter what's happened in the past. Your parents and Bobby adore you, that won't change."

"My father said those same words to me before we left to come here. I don't know if I believe him or not, but I'd like to."

"Then believe him. You're not to blame, not for one single second," I insisted.

Another hefty sigh left her petite body. A shiver shook her when the Atlantic wind zoomed over us. I clenched my shawl closer and wondered if the temperature had dropped drastically within the past half hour, or if my day had left me vulnerable to the temperature.

Stars twinkled in the dark sky overhead while the moon hung suspended like a round of cheese. Headlights and the sound of a motorcycle engine broke the peaceful night. Light laughter reached us where we sat.

Lola wiped her face with the afghan and sat up straighter in the chair. I fumbled with the shawl, draping it over my shoulders again as Marcus and Aaron drew near.

"Nana said you two were out here. From the look of you, you're both freezing. Why don't we go inside?"

I glanced up at the two dark shadows looming over us, grateful that they couldn't see Lola's distress. With a forced chuckle, I admitted we were cold, but had wanted to give Nana some peace.

"She said she's on her way to bed." Aaron's voice held a hint of question, but he never asked one.

"Then I'll go make coffee and you three can join me on the sun porch, how's that?" Lola asked and scurried off without waiting for an answer.

I called after her. "We'll be there in a minute, I want to share our adventure with the guys." It was my way of letting her know her secret was safe with me.

"What adventure?" Both men asked at once.

"Sit, and I'll tell you." Knowing I had their attention, I could draw the tale out while I gave Lola enough time to pull herself together.

They drew their chairs closer to me. It was pitch dark by this time, so we couldn't see each other's faces except for what light the moon offered. I played the story out for them, ending with my hospital treatment. Neither man spoke until I'd finished. I leaned back in the chair and waited for the questions to begin. It didn't take but a moment.

"So, another dead man, huh? Funny, Martin never said a word when we were there a while ago, though, he wasn't happy to see us. I'm glad to see you're okay," Aaron remarked.

Marcus wasn't about to be outdone. "You're sure you're all right, then? You didn't hit your head, or anything?"

I shook my head, all the while remembering Dembrotti's ghost. "I'm fine, it's only a sprained ankle. Luckily, the dead guy broke my fall, disgusting as that was. Maggots, there were maggots, did I tell you that part? Gross, very gross." I shivered for effect.

"We should go inside; you're in shock." Aaron helped me to my feet. I grabbed the crutches propped against the chair and hobbled toward the house, moving extra slow for Lola's sake.

Lamplight softened the interior of the glassed-in porch. It made the room feel warmer than it really was, though it was still warm enough to beat the evening chill.

I dropped into an overstuffed armchair while each man settled on opposite ends of the sofa. Lola brought a tray loaded with a coffee pot, cups, and a scrumptious looking cake, which she set on a coffee table. She settled into the chair nearest me, where shadows were deeper than those in the rest of the room.

Marcus noticed, but said nothing about her choice. Instead, he made an effort to ease the underlying tension in the room with sounds of appreciation that were bearlike rather than cheerful. Lola grinned at him, the atmosphere lightened, and we all spoke at once.

"Did Vin tell you of her emergency room experience? She was in so much agony, especially when the doctor bent her ankle back and forth like an old crank handle. She did well not to punch him." Her words ended on a light thread of laughter.

"He can thank his lucky stars tonight, for sure." I turned to the men and asked, "Where have you two been?"

Aaron glanced at Marcus and said, "After we saw Dave Martin, we spent time with Trooper Maddox. I was interested in finding out how the police force works over here. He's been involved in island duty for a few years, so he was able to tell us. Islanders anywhere are odd at times, and police procedure can be as well." Aaron smirked, but ended his remarks there.

Marcus picked up where Aaron left off. "I believe Martin has an axe to grind where you're concerned. First off, because you're an Italian, and secondly, because the dead man was a mobster. Now you say the other guy was killed the same way, so don't look for Martin to ease up on you, Vin." Marcus shook his head. "I can't interfere, and it's doubtful Aaron can be of help, either. Martin is a major problem as he's leading this investigation. Do you know who the second dead man was?"

I heaved a huge sigh and said, "No idea. Not yet, anyway."

# Chapter 6

We chatted until the wee hours. Lola yawned and bid us goodnight. She turned as she reached the door and asked, "You've met your quota of dead men, right, Vin?"

I failed to see the humor in her remark, but smiled and said I hoped so. She walked through the kitchen, and then I heard her light tread on the stairs.

I leaned forward and whispered, "Could you take over the investigation, Aaron, since the first guy was a mobster and the FBI always has an interest in that?" I received a shrug for my plea.

"No promises, Vin," Aaron said. "I have to wait for orders to come through. The agency is extremely interested in what's taking place out here, but like I said, no orders, no interference. Sorry."

"Okay," I said with a nod. "I guess I just have to hope things will work in my favor then."

"What's going on?" Marcus had watched Lola leave and now wanted to know more than I could tell him.

"With Lola?" I asked.

He nodded.

"She's hit a rougher patch than I'd initially thought," I said. "I can't offer up more than that. If she wants you to know, she'll tell you, so please don't ask me about it."

Marcus stared at me long and hard, while Aaron asked, "This has nothing to do with the dead bodies you found, does it?"

"No, it doesn't." I stood up and wished them a good night. "Lock up on your way out."

Marcus glanced at Aaron and muttered, "We've been dismissed."

Aaron smirked, and they left as I hobbled up the stairs.

I'd reached my room when Lola's soft voice filtered to me. "Can you come here for a minute?"

"Sure."

The small, well-appointed room was cheerful and cozy, it fit Lola's personality perfectly. I pulled a padded footstool alongside the bed and settled on it, stretching my injured ankle out after propping a pillow underneath my leg. Lola had been flipping through a magazine, probably waiting for me.

"What's up?" I asked and glanced around the sweet room. A delicate porcelain bed lamp sat atop a small round table covered with a gay patchwork patterned tablecloth that matched the curtains and comforter. Hardwood floors gleamed, and a circular, hand-braided, rug set off the color scheme.

"You didn't tell the guys what I shared with you, right?" Lola asked.

"Of course not. They were curious, but I said you'd tell them what was bothering you if you wanted them to know. I'd never speak out of turn where you're concerned, Lola."

She nodded and slumped against the headboard of the bed. "I'm not ready to talk to anyone else about it. You and Nana are the only ones I've confided in. When, and if, I'm ever ready, I'll do the telling. I might still be in pity-party mode."

" You got it." I imitated zipping my lips and Lola burst into a giggle.

With a slanted look, Lola commented, "You couldn't zip those lips if you tried, so don't make promises you can't keep. I know you won't intentionally mention my secret to Marcus and Aaron, but you do have loose lips on occasion, Vin."

"Well, it's not because I don't try to keep them zipped," I admitted with a smile.

"How do you plan to handle Martin?" Lola enquired.

I shrugged. "No clue. I'll probably wing it, like I always do. I have to watch my temper, though. Martin deliberately goads the daylights out of me, just so I'll make a mistake or blurt out information he can use against me. Since I don't have any idea what these two guys were doing out here, I can't be of much use."

I ran my hands through my heavy mane of hair. Lifting it at the roots, I massaged my scalp, and said, "Marcus can't help me much, but if Aaron can take over the investigation, then I think I'll be okay."

"Hopefully, that's what will happen." Lola was silent for a mere second before she said, "I'm sure you can handle Martin, look at how you've managed thugs and mobsters in the past. This guy should be easy."

I looked into her dark, twinkling eyes, and realized I was a lousy secret keeper. "I'll have to tread carefully, that's for sure. He would like to toss me in a cell and call it a day, but that won't solve his problem. Someone is killing off mobsters and I can't imagine who would have the nerve or reason to do it without starting an all-out war between families."

"Together, we'll deal with what comes next. I'll do all I can."

I stared at her in silence for a few seconds when an idea came forth. "How about a trip to the other end of the island tomorrow? We could drive along Corn Neck Road to the North Lighthouse and have a picnic. It would do you good. What do you say? That beach is gorgeous."

"If Officer Martin leaves you alone long enough, sure, I'd like that," Lola said with a grin. "The fridge is loaded with fruit and salad stuff, and I think there are some chicken wings, as well. That should be enough for us, don't you think?"

Encouraged by her interest, I nodded and said I'd see in her in the morning.

? ? ?

Exhaustion set in, and I must have slept like the dead, no pun intended. I awoke refreshed and ready to face the day. My renewed confidence might be put to the test, but at the moment, I was Wonder Woman.

The rattle of dishes echoed up the staircase as I left the bathroom. Fully dressed and ready to meet whatever came my way, I went to the kitchen. The swelling of my ankle had significantly decreased, and it felt better. I couldn't run or apply heavy pressure to the foot, though I could get around easier than I had.

Already at the breakfast table, Nana smiled when I entered the room.

"About time you got out of bed, sleepyhead," Nana teased. "You girls sure are night-owls."

Afraid we'd kept her awake, I began to apologize. "I'm sorry if we were noisy last night."

Nana shushed me with a wave of her hands and said she remembered what it was like to be young and have good looking men around.

I smiled and took a seat as Lola served up blueberry pancakes accompanied by warm maple syrup. Orange juice, bacon, and fresh fruit filled the center of the table. While there were only three of us, there was enough food for six people. I wondered if Lola assumed Marcus and Aaron would stop in for a meal.

Car doors slammed and the sound of voices blew through the windows on the breeze. Lola had been right in her assumption. I smiled and loaded my plate before the pancakes were gone.

"Come in," Lola called before either man had a chance to knock. She set two more plates, glasses, mugs, and additional cutlery on the table.

Nana and I were well into our feast by the time Aaron and Marcus sat down. Lola poured coffee and joined us at the table.

"What's on your agenda today?" Aaron asked.

Lola pointed to us and answered, "We're having a picnic at the North Lighthouse. Nana's getting a day of peace and quiet. What are your plans?"

"I have to work, but Aaron is going to handle Vinnie's Moped accident at the rental place this morning. A picnic sounds like a great idea, you should enjoy this weather," Marcus answered around a mouthful of pancakes.

Wide-eyed, I stared at Aaron. "You are?"

His smile widened as he said, "You were in no position to handle that last night, and the girl who operates the rental stand wasn't there when we went by just now. I'll take care of it this morning." He stared at Lola and said, "A carefree day on the beach sounds perfect."

"Thanks," I said and winked at Lola.

Nana joined in with, "I hear there's a party going on at Ballard's Inn tonight. You girls ought to check it out and have some fun." She gave Lola a meaningful look.

When the last of the food was gone, so were the two men. Nana and I cleared the table while Lola washed dishes. I dried them, and Nana put everything away while she chatted about anything that popped into her head.

I'd folded the towel and draped it over a bar attached to the cabinet when Nana looked up and said, "I believe you can get through this mess you're involved in, Vinnie. You must stay calm. And Lola, it's time you stopped feeling lost and started rebuilding your confidence. Just because your parents are too dumb to see they were made for each other, doesn't mean you're any less of a wonderful person than you've always been. People make mistakes."

The elderly woman stepped close and put her arms around Lola. "It doesn't matter who your mother had a fling with, you're a Trapezi, and you always will be, understand?"

A lone tear trickled down Lola's face as she mumbled, "Okay, Nana."

I turned away and stumbled out the door on my way to the dock. The sun was high and clouds scudded across the sky on their way to who knows where. Perched on the edge of the pier, I jumped when my cell phone jingled. My father was on the line. Oh boy.

"Hey, Dad, what's up?" I asked cheerfully.

"Is it true?"

"Is what true?" I asked as if I didn't know what he referred to.

"Dembrotti is dead?"

"He is, deader than dead, Dad. Sorry."

"He was a good man. Are you okay?"

"I am, but, Dad, I found another dead guy yesterday. The cops haven't told me who he is, and I didn't recognize him, either. He was, uh," I swallowed hard and said, "swollen and covered with maggots." I shivered and bit my lip as curiosity over my father's relationship with Dembrotti soared.

"How were they killed?" My father's voice was gruff, and I tried to picture his expression, but couldn't conjure up an image to match his voice.

"They were strangled with heavy rope. Rope that's commonly used on luxury boats. White, cord-like rope, you know the kind? Dembrotti was then thrown overboard and his body washed up in Nana Trapezi's salt marsh inlet. He was in such bad shape, I didn't recognize him."

"You're sure you're all right?" Dad asked again.

"I am. Aaron's here, and Marcus has been assigned to the island for the summer."

He scoffed. "For all the good they'll do you, just watch your back, Lavinia. No cop will ever rescue you, they'll only throw you into a cell. Be careful, trust no one. Call if you need me." The line went dead.

I gawked at the phone and stuffed it into my pocket. That was when I felt his presence and turned to glare up into Dave Martin's cold eyes.

"Was that your mob connection, Ms. Esposito?" he asked.

Was this guy a smart-mouth or what? I held my annoyance at bay and struggled to my feet. It was easier to meet someone on a near eye-to-eye level than be sitting staring upward. It was a matter of equal footing.

I answered him smoothly. "Surely, you don't believe I'm connected, Officer Martin?"

He hooked his thumbs into his belt loops, shrugged, and said, "You tell me."

I smiled. "Hmm, what brings you to Nana's?"

"You do. The second dead man has been identified as Willy "The Cheat" Conigliaro. Are you familiar with him?" Martin held out a photograph of the man when he'd been alive.

I took the photo, studied it thoroughly and handed it back with a shake of my head. "Never seen him before." Another lie added to all the others.

If Dembrotti and Conigliaro were dead, who else was on the hit list? These two men had at one time protected me from the mob when I'd gone to Federal Hill after being told not to until a certain situation had calmed down. They were racketeers for the mob. It appeared someone was cleaning house, but why? And, who? Who was killing off mobster henchmen? These thoughts raced alongside others, and flicked through my head as I watched Martin tuck the picture into his pocket.

Persistent, he asked, "You're sure you don't know either man?"

I nodded. "Very sure. I know it may be difficult for you to comprehend, being an islander and all, and non-Italian at that, but not all of us have mob ties and we don't all know one another. The majority of Italians don't like the mob any more than cops do."

"Ms. Esposito, your reputation precedes you. Police department gossip is alive and well, and I've heard about your adventures. How could I not think you're involved with the mafia on some level?"

I snickered, shook my head, and stuffed my shaking hands into the pockets of my shorts.

At that moment, Lola called out that she was ready to go and beckoned to me with a wave of her arm. I nodded and then glanced at Martin. "If you'll excuse me, I think we're done here." I went past the man and kept my limp casual, even though I wanted to run away, take the ferry to the mainland, and hide in the sanctity of my Scituate home.

Lola backed out of the small space and edged past Martin's truck. I glanced out the window to see the man make his way from the pier toward his truck with long, loping steps that reminded me of a giraffe.

As her glance flicked to me and then to the road, Lola asked, "What did Martin want?"

I sighed, opened the window and let fresh air flow in as we rode from one end of the island to the other. "He wanted to tell me the second dead guy is Willy "The Cheat" Conigliaro."

"Oh, my gosh! You've got to be kidding," Lola exclaimed loudly as she skidded to a stop on the side of the road and jammed the shift lever into park.

Shocked at her response, I said, "Not kidding. Why?"

Her eyes, wide, round and slightly scared, Lola's hands shook.

My shock turned to worry. "What's wrong?"

"Conigliaro is related to my distant cousin Rafael. You remember Rafe, don't you? They're both from a Boston mob family. Could be somebody's cleaning house."

I trembled as her words and my disbelief that she'd know the family, let alone be related to them somehow, and then to have her say what I'd been thinking, became my reality. Holy crap. Were we both in danger? Were Lola and I on the hit list? Why? Was I overreacting? Had my imagination gone on a rampage, causing me to see a ghost? Hard to tell. Things in my life could suddenly spiral out of control, and didn't that just suck? Oh, yeah.

Each of us lost in thought, we sat quietly on the side of the road for a bit before I asked, "How are you related to Conigliaro?"

"I'm not sure. My mother's great uncle or something, I think. Rafe never said, and our family never clarified it either." She turned to me, her wide eyes no longer fearful. Instead, they held a spark of anger.

"I'll get to the bottom of this, you wait and see. My mother needs to fess up, and if she knows what's good for her, she will." With that, Lola started the engine and we drove to the lighthouse for our picnic.

The lighthouse nestled close to the water's edge where waves lap the shoreline, Great White sharks often prowl the waters just off the island, and, in my opinion, anyone with any brains doesn't go swimming there. We'd parked at the end of the fenced barrier, took a beach blanket and the picnic basket from the back of the car, and ambled toward the lighthouse. The distance wasn't great, but most of the entry was blocked off by posts and guardrails, turning it into a walkway. I'd given up the use of crutches and limped a bit as we made our way forward.

The spot was beautiful and calm. We were among the few souls on the beach, though how long it would stay that way was anyone's guess. Tourists roamed Block Island end to end, and anywhere in between. All summer long they swarmed as would bees around a hive.

Waves came and went, the tide did as well, and we wiled away hours in the sunshine. I had applied a lighter wrap to my ankle before we left the house and removed it to enter the water. I waded up to my knees in the cold Atlantic and returned to shore in a limping-run with a gust of wind that pushed me along. Lola laughed when I tripped and landed hard on the warm sand. She handed me a towel, and after I'd dusted off specks of sand, a sandwich, and a glass of wine. Life didn't get better than this.

Various sized boats cruised by, one trolled for fish, and a yacht I recognized as a Benetti Delfino 93 drifted on the tide. Fascinated by the smooth, clean lines of the water craft, I recognized it as one I'd seen in the magazine Lola had brought along that featured this very boat. I flipped to the page, shielded my eyes with my hand and stared at it.

A memory niggled at me, but refused to come forward. Annoyed, I flipped the magazine closed, tossed it into Lola's carry bag, and slumped back against the low-slung beach chair.

The day cooled as the sun moved across the sky. We packed up and wandered the walkway to the car. I heard a horn, turned to peer out over the water and saw the Delfino drift toward the rocky part of the shoreline.

I shaded my eyes and said, "It looks like that boat is in trouble, Lola."

"It does, doesn't it? I'll call the marina and tell them to send out a rescue boat."

Why I hadn't thought of that, I didn't know, maybe because I was at a loss on an island. I'd always lived among mainlanders, not islanders. Lola gave the location and added her name before she said goodbye. I smiled at her and packed our paraphernalia into the car before we became enmeshed in an incident we knew nothing about. I was willing to let the rescuers handle the boat people, I had enough to worry about.

# Chapter 7

Dressed for an evening of fun, Lola and I started out on our adventure. To walk the distance wouldn't take long, but street lights were few and far between, which left lots of dark areas to stumble through, and my ankle was still a bit sore. We decided it would be best to drive to the club, and by the end of the evening we'd probably be happy to have done so.

Parked as close to the marina as we could get, we walked to Ballard's Inn, and made our way indoors for drinks. I'd just stepped away from the bar when I glimpsed Trooper Maddox on the enormous patio that extended off the back of the building. He was dressed in uniform, as was Marcus, who stood next to him.

They chatted up two gorgeous women, who naturally seemed quite taken with the uniforms, and the men that wore them. I smiled, felt not one pang of jealousy, and knew Marcus and I had done the right thing by parting. While I still cared for him, each of us had baggage that wasn't worth dealing with because compromise was impossible.

"Isn't that Marcus?" Lola asked.

"It is, and Trooper Maddox is with him. Those two good-looking women sure are admiring them." I turned to Lola and gasped softly, "I didn't look like that when Marcus came around, did I?"

Her eyes on me, Lola smiled and then laughed. "Hate to say so, but, yeah!"

I grinned, turned my gaze toward the opposite end of the patio and pointed. Lola nodded, and we set off in that direction. No questions, no murders, nothing that would ruin a chance to enjoy ourselves. If Marcus noticed us, it wouldn't be because we made it clear we had arrived.

"Not wanting any questions tonight, Vin?" Lola asked with a smile.

"It would be different to have fun for a change and not worry about being judged by anyone," I answered with a chuckle.

To our right, a party was in full swing. We mingled with the group and laughed at jokes and stories that floated through what had now become a crowd. Lola chatted with a couple of people and then was swept away on the arm of a good-looking man with a bit of a swagger. I followed them slowly, keeping an eye on Lola. These days, it was easy to be taken advantage of without knowing it was happening, especially since you could be drugged by a decent looking person.

The duo stepped off the patio and started toward a boat moored where the water was deepest at the far end of the marina. I noted it was a Delfino and wondered if it was the same boat that had been adrift earlier in the day. I kept my distance, but stayed on course when I heard a familiar voice behind me.

"Going somewhere, beautiful?" Aaron asked and clasped my hand in his.

I leaned toward him, pointed to the water craft and murmured, "Making sure Lola doesn't find herself in a bad situation. Shall we join the party on that particular boat?"

He nodded, let go of my hand and slung his arm around my shoulders as we climbed aboard. Music played, the crowd drank and danced in the open space on both decks, and I kept my eye on Lola. Short though she is, I couldn't miss that head of wild, curly, auburn hair.

Aaron and I moved closer to the couple. When the man turned, I stared, wondering why I hadn't initially recognized him. Maybe his face had been in shadow, otherwise, I'd have intervened before he'd whisked Lola away.

I nudged Aaron with my elbow and caught his attention.

"What?" he asked.

"Lola's friend, over there," I pointed, wanting to make sure I was right in my assumption. "Do you know who he is?"

"Johnny 'Boy' Pacci, a living legend in Boston. I wonder what he's doing on Block Island."

"Their conversation has become intense, don't you think? I can see signs of stress in Lola's stance."

Aaron held my arm tight when I would have started across the deck. I stopped, glanced up, and gave him a look as I murmured, "Let go."

"Not yet, Lola can handle herself, you've said as much many times. Let's see where this goes and then take action if need be."

His sound advice calmed my angst over the possibility that Lola might be in trouble. With a nod, I stepped closer to him and looked up into his eyes.

"I met John Pacci last year. Well, I didn't really meet him, I saw him with someone I knew." On occasion, Johnny Pacci played cards with my father at the Knights of Columbus Hall near my father's house. I'd never known who the man really was, or what his connection to my father might be. I'd only known him as Johnny Boy.

Aaron stared at me and asked, "Who was he with, Vin?"

With a slight shake of my head, I smiled, and said, "You know, I can't remember."

His own smile tightened a tad, but Aaron held off calling me a liar, though we both knew he was aware that I lied.

The raucous throng moved like the tide. People migrated from one end of the boat to the other as music played in tandem with waves that gently lapped the luxury craft. We were swept toward the stern with a crowd that seemed to have doubled in size. Lola was lost from sight and a skirmish had broken out on the outskirts of the lower deck where we were.

"Stay put, I'll be right back," Aaron said as he made his way into the fracas.

Eyes glued to the scene unfolding before me, I never saw the person who shoved me hard and sent me over the side and into the water. I gulped for air when I surfaced, paddled frantically to stay buoyant, and then called out.

Help wasn't forthcoming, as the skirmish had become a full-blown brawl. I treaded water, listened to people yell, and wondered what was going on. From my position, it was impossible to see what happened. Things quieted down while I searched for a way to get back onboard. I swam to the right side of the stern end of the yacht and found a step that ran alongside it with more steps leading to the first deck level. Having shifted my body onto the small step, I'd climbed the stairs when I saw Aaron's outstretched hand.

"Wet, are you?" he asked with a grin as he pulled me up to gain my balance on the deck.

"Slightly," I said sarcastically.

Three policemen and the two troopers ushered partygoers onto the wharf with a warning to keep the peace or be arrested.

"Gosh, Vinnie, you're soaked," Lola stated the obvious as she wrapped a huge towel around me, followed by a blanket. She glanced over her shoulder and said, "Let's get out of here."

The night chill permeated my clothes, and I started to tremble. I wasn't sure whether the cold caused the shaking or if I'd been worried that a shark would come in and have me for a snack. Either way, I nodded at Lola and said goodnight to Aaron, who stood aside watching her fuss over me before he glanced at Johnny Boy.

"If you're all right, I'll stop by in the morning, Vin," Aaron whispered and kissed my temple.

"K—kay, see you th—then," I stuttered and followed Lola.

We scurried along the dock, out of the wind and into the car. I tucked the blanket around me as I nestled into the seat. I glanced back at the enormous water craft and then scanned the beach beyond it. My gut tightened when I saw a pale figure with a rope hanging from his neck, beckoning me to join him. I started, tightened the blanket around my torso and said, "Get us out of here, right now."

We took off from the parking lot, as Lola asked, "What happened? You were on the deck and when I looked back, you were gone, and Aaron was breaking up the fight."

"Everyone was jostling me and then someone shoved me. The next thing I knew, I was in the ocean. Cripes, that water is cold." I shivered as Lola slowed the car to a stop in Nana's front yard and shifted into park.

Upstairs, I changed into sweatpants and a heavy sweatshirt, added warm socks and joined Lola in the cozy parlor. A crocheted granny-square afghan lay draped over the back of the sofa and I wrapped it around me. My hair was still damp and I'd gathered it into a clip.

"Feel better?" Lola asked as she poured wine into goblets.

After two hefty swigs of wine, I wiped my hand across my lips, grinned, and said, "Indeed."

Her laughter tinkled, a sweet sound similar to pieces of crystal tapping against one another. It always made me smile, and I did so now. "Who were you with onboard that yacht?"

I caught the sideways glance she slid as Lola looked anywhere but at me. I waited in silence, sort of how cops wait for you to become so uncomfortable with their silence that you open up and spill your guts to them. This wait was worth it.

Her face screwed into a grimace, Lola glanced at me, then away, and then back again. "I suppose you already know the answer to that, right?"

I said nothing, but waited.

"His name is Johnny Pacci. He plays cards with your father."

Before I could say a word, her brows hiked a notch and she said, "I played cards with him and your dad's other friends when you two were having a discussion at the K of C Hall, remember? I card sharked all four games in the time you took to straighten everything out between you. Your father walked away with nearly everyone's money because of my card playing ability. Remember now?"

Much to my dismay, I remembered and said so. "Were you aware that he's a living legend in mob circles?"

Her nod was slight, though her dark eyes sparkled in the lamplight. "He also knows my father, my *real* father. He said we look a lot alike."

In less than an instant, I'd jumped from the sofa and asked, "What? What did you say?" The afghan tumbled to the floor. I bent down, plucked it off the floor, and plunked into the chair opposite Lola. "Tell me," I said on a breath.

"Johnny saw us on the patio outside Ballard's Inn club. He said he'd heard an intriguing tidbit that he wanted to ask me about. Interested in what he had to say, and knowing you'd have my back, I agreed to go with him to his yacht. I wasn't aware until after the fist fight on deck that you were missing. You looked pretty bedraggled when you climbed out of the water." Her chuckle turned to laughter, but she cut it short when she saw my face.

What my expression held was a mystery to me because my mind was flying in directions similar to shards of glass. Except my shards were questions, lots of them. What had Johnny heard, and from whom? Who was Lola's *real* father? What did it all mean? What was his reason for taunting her? Because surely he would know his words would do so, and possibly haunt Lola if he refused to tell her. Why would anyone do such a thing to her, of all people?

"Please don't get upset, Vinnie, all is well. Johnny said he'd heard my parents were on the outs and why that had happened. He also said he saw the resemblance between me and my father when I'd fleeced him out of five hundred dollars at the card table that night. I got a kick out of taking their money, Vin. It was so easy."

Who was this stranger sitting across from me? And, what had she done with the real Lola? The Lola that I knew would have been horrified by the evening's happenings. Instead, this woman seemed to embrace her new persona and had decided to toss out the old one. Gracious, could she have lost her marbles?

Tentatively, I asked, "Lola, are you sure you're okay?"

"I've never felt better," she answered. "All my life I felt I had to prove my worth to my family. My father was hard on me if I didn't get perfect grades. My mother, who will answer my questions or else, never interfered with my father for haranguing me, she always defended his actions by saying he wanted me to achieve the best I could. I never understood what she meant until tonight. They were afraid I'd be like my *real* father." She spoke so matter-of-factly that all I could do was to gawk at her.

Finally, I murmured, "I'm sure that's not true."

"Think about it, I was the child of another man, a mobster, for goodness sake. As those men are, he must be a man with no scruples and a lack of conscience. My parents didn't want me to end up like that." Lola shrugged. "In all honesty, maybe they did me a favor by acting the way they did while I grew up, but that's over. I have my own life, and I'll do anything I damn well please now. My mother always worried that I would become entangled in your mob adventures. Now we know why, right?"

Slowly, I nodded since what Lola said made sense in my addled brain. I was shocked and somewhat appalled by this new Lola. She hadn't lost her marbles, and I worried that maybe this was a bad dream. If so, somebody should wake me before it got worse.

After another glass of wine, I knew I'd wished the whole thing was a bad dream, including the ghost of Dembrotti. Lola said Johnny Boy wouldn't say who her father was, but had hinted that she should go yachting with him so they could talk privately.

I shook my head so violently my hair clip flew to the floor. "You'll go nowhere without me, do you understand? Somebody is offing people, and I refuse to allow you to be one of them. I'll not breathe a word of this to anyone, not Aaron or Marcus, but you have to promise not to go with Johnny or his *friends,* without me tagging along."

"Sure thing," Lola said calmly.

Gone was the woman who had taken the news of her parentage as though she'd been at fault. Gone was the sad, depressed, woman who had worried me to no end. Gone was the chef who minded her own business. Now she was replaced with a stranger who'd stepped up and would take everything as a challenge. Lola had stiffened her spine, lifted her chin, and decided she would do what she wanted, rather than what was expected of her. Oh boy.

A nickname given to her by Marcus suddenly popped into my head. He'd always referred to her as *Little Miss Dynamite*. Had he recognized a quality in Lola that I had missed all these years? She'd been a willing partner in my escapades, but never in as forthright a manner as she had now.

I leaned back in the chair and studied this firebrand with new eyes. Lola wanted to move forward, take what was thrown her way, and make the challenge worthwhile. I smiled at the thought of her standing in my shoes when things went awry, and then wondered if she would handle those situations better than I ever could. I gave a slight snort and thought better of the idea.

Some time ago, when mobster Tony Jabroni had been stabbed and Lola had stumbled across him, she'd looked at me, her face pure white, and asked how I dealt with incidents such as those.

Curious over this new Lola, I asked, "What are you considering?"

"That I will get the information I want, use it the way I see fit, and then I'll let you know what's next."

"What's the plan, exactly?"

"We're going yachting with Johnny sometime in the near future." She raised her hand as I opened my mouth. "I'm not changing my mind, so if you're about to try and dissuade me, don't bother. Either you're in or you're not. Which is it?"

"Whew, I feel like the tables have been turned. Usually, it's me asking you to join the adventure, but this time, it's you doing the asking.

Would I ever not satisfy my overabundant curiosity?" I laughed and added, "Count me in, definitely in."

While I'd decided to partner up with Lola to try and keep her safe, I wondered what my Dad would say if I asked him who Lola's father was. Would he deny knowing? Likely. Would he tell me to mind my business? Probably. Would he eventually divulge the truth behind her parentage? Never. I sipped more wine, felt the buzz it left me with, and relaxed a bit more.

A companionable silence lengthened between us as we finished our wine. Lola said she would see me in the morning, and I nodded, comfortable from the warmth the afghan offered. I watched her leave the room, tread up the stairs, then I heard the click of her bedroom door closing.

I snuggled deeper into the chair, allowing my mind to run its course where curiosity and what-ifs were concerned. Never in a million years could I have imagined Lola to be in this position, nor would I have thought she'd handle the idea of her illegitimacy quite so well. Like most surprises in life, there were good and bad sides to them.

# Chapter 8

Wind tumbled my hair as Johnny Boy's yacht moved from the bay into deep waters. Sunny skies had been the norm until unexpected gray skies moved in, threatening rain. I watched Lola take stock of our surroundings.

The interior of the Delfino's first level was stunning, while the upper deck interior was even more so. Rich colors, soft leather, and thick carpets revealed no expense had been spared where this luxurious water craft was concerned. From stem-to-stern, ninety-something feet of elegance surrounded us. I relished the beauty of gleaming mahogany bar and the subtle, sunken lighting above our heads, everything was streamlined and rich looking, even though my spidey sense told me to take care and remain cautious.

A moment later, Johnny nonchalantly strolled in. An inch or so shorter than I am, I studied the man of Boston Mafia fame. His hair was only slightly laced with gray at the temples, making him look younger than he was. Expensive Italian leather sandals adorned feet that were better manicured than mine, and he was quite fit, with no excess fat lolling around his middle. Confidence exuded from him as he idly crossed the thick span of carpet to sit on a leather lounge close to Lola's chair. All the man needed were two slaves waving palm fronds above his head to keep him cool.

A brawny man stood just inside the door, his feet apart and his hands clasped lightly in front of him. His face passive, his eyes held a cold gleam, and he was the epitome of a bodyguard with no qualms about killing someone who might dare harm his boss.

One of the wait staff brought in a tray loaded with beverages and foods to nibble. I stayed put as he poured drinks, served them, and then offered snacks that were more than peanuts and chips. Lobster bites, shrimp, Italian and Greek olives, cheese, and more, tempted me. Oh yeah, this was the life.

My inner voice chose that moment to nag me. *You say that now, but what if you and Lola are tossed overboard and served up as shark chum. What then? Smarten up, Vinnie.* Okay, the voice was on a rant, and I was damned if I could find a way to shut it off. With a tiny sigh, I sipped the best tasting margarita ever and watched the interaction between Lola and Johnny Boy.

She offered up the Julia Roberts smile and got the usual reaction, which paved the way for the question upper most on her mind. "You said you know my father? Would you mind telling me how you know him?"

His dark-eyed stare hadn't left her features since he'd entered the room. Johnny studied Lola as if he saw her, really saw her, for the very first time. Then he grinned amiably.

"Is it so important to you, Lola?"

"Wouldn't you want to know the name of your father, Johnny?" she countered.

His facial features stiffened for a heartbeat before he said, "There was a time when that was the only thing I wanted to know. It was the most important thing in my life. I was consumed by the need to know his name and where he was, until I realized what was truly important."

Shaken by his admission of not knowing his own father, and her faux pas, Lola's eyes widened and she asked softly, "And what was that?"

"The important thing was what I did in life that mattered most. Isn't that what your family preaches to you, to this day, Lavinia?" He glanced at me and then looked back at Lola. "Don't you agree, Lola? It's not where you came from, but who you are, and what you accomplish that counts in this life. We only have one life," he said with a snicker and tipped his head toward me. "Unless you're Miss Esposito, of course." His glance landed on me and then flicked away. "You seem to have more lives than a cat."

I'd watched the two of them size each other up as Johnny spoke and wondered what the meaning was behind his statements. It was apparent he was also illegitimate.

Today, it wasn't as big of a deal to be born on the wrong side of the sheets as it would have been back in the day, when Johnny was a child. Disrespected and shunned would have been the norm for him. I envisioned him as a kid, being treated as such, and my heart squeezed with sadness. It was then that I guessed his age was not that far from my dad's, who was in his early sixties.

I couldn't imagine a lifetime of disrespect and thought again of how he'd managed to get through it. My inner voice piped up. *Don't get all soft and gushy about this guy, he's a bum, a thug, a mafia don, for goodness sake.* I shivered a bit at the truth of it. He was all of those things, and presumably more.

"Isn't that right, Lavinia?"

Lost in thought, I nearly jumped out of my skin when Johnny said my name. I nodded until I felt like a bobble-head doll. I'd set my glass and snack plate aside when my phone jingled. I excused myself and strode onto the open end of the deck while my father went on about the dead guys. When he took a breath, I said, "Dad, wait. Begin again."

"Where are you, Lavinia? It sounds like a hurricane is blowing."

"I'm boating on the ocean. The wind is blowing steadily. What's the matter?"

"You need to watch yourself. I've heard about the dead men and I'm very upset, especially since you're there and can never mind your business."

This was it. I was going to get the usual lecture. I looked upward and rolled my eyes as I paced the deck, all the while making a silent promise to hold my temper.

"Why are you so nervous? You never get nervous."

"You make me jittery. Actually, you make me a wreck."

"If you don't tell me what's on your mind, I won't know how to handle a situation, should one arise. Right now, I'm intent on keeping Lola's mental marbles in one bag and helping her through this trying time. What have you heard?"

"That's good of you. Lola's gonna need your strength."

Okay, enough tap dancing. I wanted an answer and my father would give it to me, no matter what it took for me to wring it out of him.

"Who is her father?" I demanded in a no-nonsense tone.

"I can't say, but I've heard he's on the island, so be careful and don't push your luck, understand? I can't intervene on your behalf while you're both on an island in the damn Atlantic Ocean.

"Okay, okay, don't get a knot in your knickers. Repeat what were you saying about the dead men? Why were Dembrotti and Conigliaro murdered?"

"There have been some business struggles lately. Dembrotti and Conigliaro were caught in the middle of them. That's why I'm worried about you two. The mob is on, or near, the island and there's bound to be trouble."

I caught my breath. "The policeman investigating those deaths is bugging the daylights out of me, but so far, I haven't been arrested. The jerk keeps asking if I'm connected, and it's all I can do not to toss him into the marsh."

"Keep your wits about you. That's all I can say. Tell the cops nothing, admit to nothing, and if you need a lawyer, call me."

The line went dead. I shook the phone and said hello four or five times before I realized he'd hung up. *Geesh, that's rude.*

I turned and stared into the hard, cold eyes of a broad shouldered, barrel chested thug who had taken a Superman stance not five feet away from me. My feet weighed a ton as I trudged past him. Maybe my brain envisioned ankles shackled in chains and feet covered with cement for overshoes. I'm not sure, but it took courage for me to give him a brief nod and walk by into the salon where Lola and Johnny were chuckling over a remark he'd made.

Johnny's eyes lit on me and he beckoned me to join them. "Lavinia, come join us for lunch. The chef has prepared a wonderful meal that you'll both enjoy."

"Lovely idea, can't wait," I said with a smile that I'm certain didn't quite convince anyone.

Lola's eyes seemed troubled as she looked up at me while we followed Johnny into a spacious room appointed with nothing but the best accoutrements that money could buy. I glanced away from Lola and gave Johnny a winning smile as I complimented him on the yacht and its décor. It was my turn to be charming and give Lola a rest. After all, I was more adept at this than she was.

His smile was one of pride as he glanced around. "I hired a guy to come in and decorate the place for me. He has a good eye for detail, don't you think?"

"Absolutely. As a matter of fact, you have two paintings over there that were done by an artist I know." I pointed to and admired Lanky Larry's work. I viewed the room with renewed interest in the décor. Larry and I had worked together on a couple of artistic projects some time ago. His talent was unquenchable and nonstop.

Johnny tapped his lip with his index finger and thought a moment before saying, "His name is Larry. Can't remember the last name, but he's a short, bald, chubby guy. I wasn't aware you were friends." His eyes glinted, and I wondered if he considered checking up on me through Larry. The last thing I wanted was to involve Larry in any issues Lola and I might face, or for this man to know that I'd helped put Tony Jabroni and his miserable wife in jail.

"I met him in college and we've stayed in touch," I said. It wasn't a lie, not exactly.

Seated at the round, glass and steel table, I was on Johnny's left and Lola sat on his right. Lobster and sea scallops were the fare, along with the tastiest whipped, twice-baked potatoes I'd ever eaten. A crystal bowl of salad greens, sprinkled with light vinaigrette, was passed back and forth between Lola and me, while Johnny Boy smiled and bragged about his yacht.

My mind wandered a tad before I focused again. Could this be the last supper—our last supper? I rejected the thought as it tumbled through my brain, though with the look Lola had given me on our way in, I wondered if I was on track with the last supper idea.

"I saw you at the Knights of Columbus Hall with my father. How long have you known him?" I asked while our server removed plates and glassware, and replaced them with dessert and espresso.

"We've played cards together for years, but I knew him long before that, Lavinia. He's a good man, your father."

Though I hadn't planned to, I blurted, "How long is long?"

"I don't actually remember when we met, why do you ask?" His eyes had taken on a cool gleam and his features were bland as he stared at me.

I'd seen that look on other thugs and was aware that I had entered secret territory. I'd get no truthful answer, I was certain of it.

"Just wondering. Dad plays cards with a regular crew of cronies, but I've only seen you there once, uh, not that I go to the hall often or anything." I'd gone from blurting to bumbling, so I shoveled cheesecake into my mouth to resist speaking another word.

His light chuckle intimidated me more than if he'd done a monster bwa-ha-ha. Chills raced along my skin as would snow, drifting on the wind. It was clear I wasn't ready to know what my father's association was, or is, or ever would be, to the mob.

"We met at a family party when I was younger. A christening of sorts as I recall," Johnny said softly. His eyes glazed in remembrance, at least I thought it was such. It lasted a moment or two before he tossed his napkin on the table and rose when the thug from the deck came over and handed him a note.

"If you'll excuse me, this is important. Antonio will get anything else you require." His features cold, Johnny Boy strode purposefully from the room, slammed the door, and was gone.

Lola and I exchanged looks, glanced at Antonio, the thug, and then we left the table. We scurried outside into the light mist of rain that sprinkled gently upon us. My curiosity ratcheted up to an unexpected level and my inner voice chimed in. *Don't get any wild ideas. You and Lola are at a disadvantage on open water. Remember this, you could be fish food. Don't be an idiot.*

When we took the steps to the lower deck and stood under the overhang, out of the rain, Lola asked, "What do you think that was about?"

With a shrug, I said, "Could be anything, but I sure would like to return to dry land. There are some aspects of Johnny Boy that we need to discuss in private. We also need to come up with a plan to get the information you seek, since you definitely didn't get it while I was on the phone with my father."

"Vin, you don't think Johnny and your father are mobsters, do you? I mean, Johnny definitely is, but I refuse to believe that of your dad."

I stared at her, saw the plea in her eyes and knew she'd faked the entire rough and tough attitude accompanied by the devil-may-care spirit she'd engaged in earlier. Lola was the same woman I'd always known, the only difference being that her determination to learn the truth had deepened.

"My father is not a mobster, he is not connected, and I'm glad you don't think he is. What he does have are favors owed him by certain people. That's what I want to believe and what I will believe. He warned us to be smart and to stay alert while we're on the island, so be careful what you ask and how you do so. I don't want to end up a floater like Dembrotti or as a raccoon's snack like Conigliaro."

"What else did he say? I can tell you're holding something back, Vin," Lola said.

Reluctantly, I answered her. "He mentioned the mob is on the island, or near it, and that he fears trouble will follow, which has already begun. Dad also said your father was reported to be here, but he refused to tell me his name."

Lola gasped. "He knows who my father is? He's known for how long?"

"Sorry, he didn't say. It's easier to pin him down when he's standing in front of me. The phone gives him the opportunity to hang up when he's had enough of my questions. What did Johnny have to say while I spoke with my father?"

She opened her mouth, then snapped it shut when she caught sight of our host advancing toward us.

"You girls will be soaked if you stay out here too much longer. Come in, come in," he crooked his fingers in a come-hither motion and slid the doors closed after we entered the lower level room.

"I'm sorry we have to cut our visit short, but I have business to address and must return to the island immediately. You've both been wonderful guests, and I've enjoyed having you on board. Let's do this again soon, shall we?"

I'd glanced out the wide side-view windows as he spoke and noticed we'd never been far from land now the fog and rain had disappeared, and that the foggy mist had covered the shoreline, leaving it invisible. Relief washed over me when I considered our return to port. Thankful for it, I smiled and gushed over our time spent with Johnny and his crew. When I fell silent, Lola picked up and did her fair share of schmoozing.

The anchor dropped, lines were secured, and we disembarked with many thanks to our host. Johnny's bodyguard, the thug who'd kept an eye on all that went on, stared impersonally at us as we waved goodbye to his boss. *A cold-blooded killer, my voice said* and then fell silent as I agreed with a mental *uh, huh.*

We walked along the waterfront admiring sailboats and other water crafts. Aaron stood at the end of the pier, his face a mask of disbelief.

# Chapter 9

"Hey there," I greeted Aaron with a smile that was met by a scowl. Lola stood at my side and glanced around. It was clear she didn't plan to enter into conversation with him in case he gave us a difficult time.

"What do you think you're doing hanging out with Johnny Pacci?" Aaron demanded.

"We were invited onto his yacht and accepted his hospitality. What's the harm in that?" I asked, fully knowing I walked a thin line.

When he stepped between Lola and me, took each of us by an elbow, and propelled us away from the dock, it was certain we were in for trouble. "Let's get out of here, we need to talk," he snapped.

Silently, the three of us moved along the beach, a few feet back from the water's edge and found an empty spot to hunker down and chat. Puffy clouds billowed across the blue sky, the beach sand was now dry from the glaring sun, and most of the tourists were in the water. I glanced up at Aaron and waited.

"I've searched high and low for the two of you. What were you thinking, Vinnie?" he groused with a stern look.

"I've explained and won't say it again. Can we move on? What are you upset about? "

A sigh and shake of his head showed his frustration with the two of us. Fleetingly, guilt rolled over me before I stiffened my spine.

About to speak, I noticed Lola's small shake of her head as she tucked her hand into Aaron's and said, "Come, walk with me. I'll explain why we were on the yacht."

Settled onto the soft sand, I watched the way he towered above her as they walked away. I heard her say, "I need information and plan to get it, no matter what I have to do."

Her words brought a smile to my lips, but fear roiled in my stomach at the thought of what it might take, and what could happen to us

63

should we venture into shark-filled mafia waters. Those types of sharks don't have fins, but are just as cold and deadly.

When they returned, Aaron was the quiet one, while Lola's face held satisfaction. I wasn't sure what she'd said, but Aaron's eyes were troubled. I rose, brushed sand from my clothes, and stepped toward them when a police car pulled to a stop at the edge of the road. Martin sat behind the wheel, staring coldly in my direction. Good grief.

With a slight wave of my hand and a smile, I waited for him to shuffle through the sand and stop in front of me.

"Miss Esposito, you need to come with me," he said.

"Why?"

"I have more questions and would like to ask them at the station rather than on a public beach."

"What do you want to know now? Do I need a lawyer? Has there been another death?" The words tumbled out one after the other as panic quickened my pulse and breathing became difficult.

"Just come with me and all will be made clear," Martin ordered as he took my arm.

When his fingers began to tighten, I pulled away from his hold. "I don't plan to go anywhere until I know what this is about, is that clear enough for you?" I asked.

Dave Martin stepped close to me and murmured, "This morning you were seen in the company of a known criminal, Miss Esposito. I want to know what you were doing with him, and you too, Miss Trapezi." He gave her a quick glance and then focused on me again.

"That would be none of your business, Officer Martin. We weren't breaking the law, so run along," Lola remarked as she stared at him. "It's a free country, and we'll see anyone we want."

Annoyance rolled across his face, his cheeks flushed, and Dave Martin's eyes snapped with anger. He knew, just as we did, that he couldn't force us to answer his questions. No laws had been broken, even though we'd made a poor decision to hang out with Johnny Boy.

His glare fierce, Martin said, "I'll be back, Miss Esposito, and when I am, you'll answer all my questions, understand?"

"You come back anytime you want, but don't expect my cooperation on any level, understand?" I returned.

In a snit, Martin stomped through the sand and drove away.

Aaron shook his head in dismay.

I gawked at him and asked, "What?"

"You really know how to make enemies, Vin."

I shrugged. "He was never an ally."

"True, but did you have to antagonize him further?"

I shuffled my feet in the sand and turned to stare out over the ocean. Block Island was an idyllic place to spend the summer, too bad our visit had become marred by two dead bodies, constant badgering by the police department, and fearsome mobsters who lingered just offshore on yachts.

Abruptly, I trudged off the beach and walked up the country road toward Nana's house. My ankle was sore, and I wanted some peace from those who would badger me until I lost my temper. Lola and Aaron chatted as they followed along behind me.

In no mood for company, I reached the house and veered out onto the dock where a beach chair sat empty and waiting. I flopped into it, studied the landscape, and leaned my head back, allowing the sun to warm my skin. As the breeze drifted across the marsh, I considered all that had happened during our brief stay on the island.

The fact that Marcus and Aaron were here, and Lola had decided to buck up and show some spirit by way of taking on the mob to get the information she wanted, did nothing to encourage me to relax. Instead, my nerves whined like a taut violin string that was ready to snap. Then there was always the ghostly form of Dembrotti, that it seemed, was only visible to me. No one else had mentioned seeing his ghost, and the sight of the man gave me the willies.

How did I get involved in these messes? Why me? No answers readily available, I slapped my hand on the arm of the chair in anger. Dang, this business was annoying. Soft footsteps sounded on the pier, and I turned in the chair.

Lola unfolded a beach chair, then set it next to mine. "Are you done being angry yet?"

"Not really. I just don't know how I get wrapped up in these affairs. Quite honestly, it's pissing me off."

"It's not as if you ask for trouble, Vin. It seems to find you," Lola said with a light chuckle.

"It does, doesn't it? What explanation did you give Aaron when you two went walking?" Curiosity was my enemy, but my need to know was severe.

Her laughter drifted on the breeze and caused me to smile.

I glanced at her and remarked, "Well?"

"I told him what had brought me to the island, what I had found out about my father so far, and then listened to a lecture on staying clear of the mob. I understand why you dread those little talks that Aaron, Marcus, and your father, bombard you with. They treat you like you're a witless idiot. No wonder you behave the way you do, and I don't mean that in a bad way," Lola said with a grin.

"Finally, somebody who gets it. Before you joined me just now, I was wondering what I did to deserve the situations I'm constantly involved in. I haven't come up with any answers to my questions, though. I guess my curiosity is a huge part of the problem, and then there are surprises like Conigliaro and Dembrotti. You know, Dembrotti was kind enough to protect me at a time when I truly needed it, a time when I had no idea who my enemy really was. I'm a bit sad that he's met his maker."

"He was a thug. Of course he'd meet a terrible end." Lola shrugged and spread her hands to study her fingernails. "I suppose dying the way he did is better than having prostate cancer."

I laughed out loud. "I don't believe you just said that. What's happened to the real Lola? Have aliens kidnapped her, or what? A few months ago, you'd never have considered saying such a thing."

Laughter lit her face, and the angst she'd been carrying seemed to vanish in that moment.

"I guess you're right, but after becoming involved in the Tim Slaggard and Frankie Tomatoes adventure, I guess my outlook on life began to change. Now that I know my father is alive and a mobster, I tend to view life a bit differently. I refuse to run away and hide from whatever comes to light, though I won't necessarily embrace it either. Rest assured, the aliens have nothing to do with it."

The clack of heels against the wooden pier brought us around with a start. Lola's grandmother waved the phone as though air-drying it. When she drew closer, she called, "Lola, your mother is on the line. She needs to speak with you right away, she says it's important."

The chair tumbled sideways as Lola jumped up to take the call. Her face blanched, her eyes widened, and a blanket of fear began to suffocate me in a terrifying way. I leaned sideways, righted Lola's chair, and waited for her to explain when she ended the call.

"My gangster father wants to meet with Mom, and she wants me to return home immediately. What do you think, Vin?"

I waffled a bit, not wanting to be left on the island alone, and not willing for Lola to leave without me. After all, she might need my support. Unsure if I'd be arrested if I tried to return to the mainland, I said, "I'll call Aaron and my father, then we'll figure out our next step, okay?"

Lola gave me a nod, returned to her chair and plunked into it while handing me the phone. I waved it away, withdrew my cell phone from my pocket, and speed dialed Aaron.

He answered on the first ring. I made short work of what had happened and listened intently as he said he'd try to clear the path for me to leave the island. All said, I hadn't committed any crimes so no one could hold me against my will. Relieved to hear he supported my right to leave, I agreed and then dialed my father. His gruff voice echoed in my ear.

"What's going on out there, Lavinia?" Dad asked.

I repeated what I'd told Aaron and waited for Dad's opinion. The wait seemed to last forever, but he eventually said, "You'd better come back with Lola." The line went dead. Aggravated by the way he had hung up on me, I shook the small instrument and then said to Lola, "Let's pack up. We can get the ferry if we're quick about it."

That was when Dave Martin put a crimp in our plans. He'd driven into the yard and parked while we were talking. He walked onto the pier and said, "I hope you're both in a better frame of mind, because you're coming to the station with me."

Lola stared at him for a second and said, "Sorry, I have to return home. Family emergency."

"You'll not leave the island unless there's been a death in your family. That goes for you, too, Ms. Esposito," Martin said as he shifted his gaze from Lola to me.

I leaned toward Lola and whispered, "Let's do what he says. Call your mother and invite her here. I don't think Martin would allow us to leave even if the President himself called and ordered it."

"Right." Lola gave Martin a sly glance and said, "Fine, let's go, then. I have things to attend when I get back." She marched off with a stiff spine and a no-nonsense attitude, leaving Martin and me staring after her.

We'd climbed into the SUV and rode to the police station after Nana was asked to call Lola's mother and tell her to come to the island. The ride was short, not sweet, but tense, instead.

Settled in chairs in front of Martin's desk, Lola and I waited for him to ask the questions neither of us wanted to answer.

"Is it true that you are friends with John Pacci?" Martin asked me.

"We aren't friends, he simply invited me and Lola out for an afternoon on his boat," I answered softly.

"Are either of you aware of his mob ties?"

Innocently, we looked at each other and I said, "We had no idea. Now that you mention it, though, I was surprised by the men on his boat. They were like bodyguards and didn't speak to us."

Martin's expression indicated his disbelief and he asked, "Were you ever aware the mob had come to the island for some type of brotherhood gathering?"

"Not a clue. Why would we be privy to that information?"

"I'll ask the questions, Ms. Esposito. You two are on dangerous ground here. The mob is not likely to be happy when they realize you were the one who found the dead men."

As uneasy as I was, I shrugged with false nonchalance and said, "I didn't kill them, so their deaths have nothing to do with me."

He turned his attention to Lola and smiled at her. The old Lola might have fallen for his act, but the new, savvier, Lola never would.

"Lola, your friend could get you killed. And what about your grandmother, what will she think of all this?"

"We aren't in danger of being killed. As for my grandmother, you should ask her that question., I can't read her mind."

A muscle at his jaw line began to flex and anger wasn't far from the surface as I watched Martin's attitude change. The real cop came forward, and there'd be no more Mr. Nice Guy.

"I can't save you from the mob if you refuse to cooperate," Martin snapped.

"We can't cooperate if we don't know anything," I returned defiantly.

"That's all you'll say, then?"

"That's it, we have no idea what the mob is up to, we have no information to share, and even if we did, it would likely be deadly for us to do so," I answered as I left the chair and motioned to Lola to do the same.

Lola gave him a dazzling smile and said, "Just so you know, we'll be at Nana's for another day. Then we'll be returning to the mainland."

Martin gave us a cold stare and said as he stared at me, "You'll leave the island when I say you can. There's an ongoing investigation in the deaths of two men that you, Ms. Esposito, are involved in. It's imperative that you remain close by should there be questions I need answers to. You can go now."

We both gave Martin a nod and walked out of the station. I guessed asking for a ride back to Nana's was out of the question. We'd rounded the corner and found Aaron's Yukon parked on the side of the road. He leaned against the front fender, his arms crossed, awaiting us.

"Are you here to rescue us?" I asked.

"Get in," he ordered.

I glanced at Lola and we readily scrambled into his truck. He drove to the other end of the island and parked at the lighthouse entrance.

We got out, walked the grounds in silence and settled on the cliff wall. Aaron stared out over the water for a while. Lola and I remained silent, waiting for him to begin yammering at us about sailing with the mob. Imagine our surprise when he didn't berate us for our actions.

"You two can help me out with Johnny Boy, if you're interested, that is. I've been handed the job of finding out why the mob is on the island and why they chose this as the site for their get together. Are you interested?"

"Will you be acting in your mob-related capacity?" I asked.

Aaron nodded. "I may not be able to come to your aid should you be caught out, Vin. You'll have to be careful, very careful. Pacci's no fool, and while he knows your father, that might not help you either."

Before I could contain it, I gasped at his words. He was aware my father and Johnny knew one another. Well, damn.

"How long have you known about my father and Johnny?"

"Not long. Any idea what that's about?"

I shook my head. "I just know they play cards together on occasion. Acquaintances from back in the day, I'd guess."

"Lola, do you know anything you'd care to share?"

Lola glanced at me and said, "I played cards with Johnny once, took him for five hundred dollars, and never saw him again until the other night."

Aaron laughed. "You stole five hundred bucks from him?"

Lola snickered and admitted, "I card sharked him and a bunch of other guys that Mr. E. plays cards with. I think they let me get away with it by saying I had beginners luck."

"You're not a beginner, though, are you?"

"Not at all. My portion of payment for college was by playing cards with the rich kids."

His eyes wide, Aaron shook his head, and said, "I'd never have guessed."

# Chapter 10

The ferry drew into port and docked. Cars slowly disembarked as passengers walked across the lot. Anxiously, we awaited Lola's mother and waved when she glanced around looking for us. She gave us a slight smile, slung an overnight bag onto her shoulder, and joined us.

Her brown eyes crinkled at the corners when she smiled, her blonde-streaked, brown, shoulder-length hair blew frantically in the wind. We gave her hugs before we climbed the steps to Lola's Cooper. Inside the car, she shook her head, and finger combed her hair to regain control of it. I smiled, knowing that would never happen, I'd been fighting that losing battle since my own arrival.

"You had an uneventful ferry crossing, then?" I asked as I settled in the back seat.

"Yes, the trip was fine, thanks," Eve answered. She turned her head toward Lola and asked, "Why did you ask that I come here?"

"It's a long story, but I figured you'd be better off with us at your side than being alone."

"You could have come home, Lola."

"No, Mom, I couldn't. I have to stay on the island for a while."

When Lola glanced at me in the rearview mirror, I guessed she was reluctant to own up to why we couldn't leave.

"We need to have a private conversation, Lola," Eve said softly.

"You know what, Mom, Vinnie is aware of everything, so you can speak freely in front of her. There have been enough secrets kept, and I want everything out in the open. Really, Mom, a gangster?"

Eve's features hardened, and she said, "I'd prefer it if you didn't speak to me in that tone, dear."

"Get used to it, Mom. I'm done tiptoeing around everyone and being left to feel that I'm not good enough for anything."

An indrawn breath, audible even from the backseat of the tiny car, was Eve's answer. We'd arrived at Nana's by then, and I left the two women sitting together in the car. My spot on the dock beckoned me, and I couldn't get there fast enough. Sure there'd be words between the two women, I wanted no part of it. Whatever happened now should stay between them, until Lola wanted to share it with me, that is.

Sprawled on the dock, under the warmth of the sun, I heard the sound of raised voices from the open windows of the car. Unable to understand what was being said, I turned my head toward the spot where Lola had parked and saw her and Eve arguing. Hand movements alone said the conversation wasn't going well. Italians tended to talk with their hands, making wild gestures, and such. This was an undeniable case of it.

The screen door slapped shut and, brought on the wings of a breeze, the sound echoed across the water. I watched Nana approach the car, swing the passenger door open, and motion for Eve to get out. *Oh, my.* I rose from the deck and went to meet the group.

Her dark brown eyes snapped with anger and her freckled face was flushed as Lola stood next to me. She leaned in and whispered, "Gee, thanks for deserting me."

I whispered back, "The new Lola handled herself very well. Good job."

She shot me a swift glance and I laughed, causing her to grin. Rooted to the spot, we waited for Eve to pull her bag from the backseat. She accompanied Nana into the house, followed slowly by Lola and me. With grievances aired, the argument had ended, and all was peaceful, at least for the moment.

Nana motioned to a chair. "Sit, I'll pour some wine, Eve. Are you hungry? I have some nice cannoli from the bakery. Would you care for one?"

Not to insult her hostess, Eve said she'd enjoy a pastry and the wine would be perfect. It would never do to say no when offered food or a beverage, even if you didn't want it. It's an Italian thing, for sure. I smiled, knew Nana had things under control and would continue to do so, if it killed everyone in the interim.

"You two must come to an agreement over your differences, with understanding on both sides. Lola is upset to find that she's been lied to all these years, and you, Eve, have lied to her for a very long time." When Eve looked as though she'd say something, Nana continued speaking.

"I'm not saying either of you are wrong, what I want to see is open communication between you. No throwing accusations and insults around, it's way too late for that." Nana looked at Lola and said, "Eve has been a good mother all these years, remember that." She then turned her gaze to Eve and said, "It's time for honesty, an all-out-in-the-open honesty." Her gaze skillfully passed over me, her slight wink nearly unnoticeable.

The wine and cannoli disappeared while stilted conversation began between mother and daughter.

I rose, cleared the table and said I'd happily make dinner. Nana agreed to help, and the two of us began the ritual of peeling veggies while Lola and her mother ironed out their issues.

To my surprise and pleasure, the new Lola held her ground, contained her anger and angst, and allowed Eve to explain her actions. I tried hard not to listen, but of course, the kitchen was small and my ears were trained on the two women.

With veggies on the grill and fish wrapped in foil next to it, I worked outside while Nana set the table. Eve had gone upstairs to shower and change. Lola wandered the grounds and then came back to see me while I played chef-du-jour. She said they'd gotten many of the issues, concerning her parents, and her mobster dad, out of the way.

Relieved that Lola had taken the opportunity to talk things through, I held up my glass of wine and saluted her. "If anyone could do it, I knew it would be you. What's going to happen with your real father? Will your mother go to see him?"

"I'm not sure where that's going, but I did tell her the dons had chosen to meet on the island for some reason. You know, Vin, I wonder if they think the FBI can't monitor them as well here as they can on land?"

"What?" I asked and stared at her.

"I was thinking of boats all looped together in open water like party boats do and how difficult it might be for the FBI to listen in on everyone." She chortled and watched to see if I got the picture. I did and smiled.

"Imagine the amount of partying that could take place and what it would be like to follow all the conversations?" I flipped the foiled fish over and turned the veggies for even cooking. From the house, I heard Nana call out, "The salad is done." I said we'd be in shortly.

"You could get used to life on this island, couldn't you, Vin?" Lola asked.

Wide-eyed and cautious, I said, "Uh, no, not really. The wind blows constantly, temperatures drop dramatically at night, and I'd freeze my butt off in the winter. No, I think not, why? Are you considering a move out here?"

"No, I just saw how you worship the sun on the dock, watch the sunrise every morning, and you flip that spatula like nobody's business." She chortled, turned, and entered the house before I could comment. Not long afterward, I went inside with a platter of grilled food.

A truck pulled into the yard. Aaron meandered into the kitchen and seemed to fill the room. I did mention it was a small kitchen, right? Nana smiled in greeting and motioned to a chair as Lola and I chimed a hello. Eve sat with a perplexed expression on her face.

"Eve, I'd like you to meet my tenant, Aaron Grant," I said.

She gave him a nod, and he gave her a winning smile as he walked over to give Nana a peck on the cheek. It was easy to see Nana was hooked by his charm and good looks.

Eve's brows rose, and she asked, "Your tenant?"

"Yes, one with no benefits," I whispered with a grin.

Her laughter was soft, her eyes disbelieving, Nana and I set the meal on the table and sat down to eat.

Dinner was gone in less time than it took to cook it. Neither Lola nor I mentioned Aaron was an undercover FBI agent, and rightly so in the light of Eve's prior relationship with a mobster.

? ? ?

The sun sank below the horizon while Lola, Aaron, and I lounged around the fire pit discussing the day's events. Nana and Eve had called it a night and went to bed after watching her favorite comedy on television. I clutched the tightly knit afghan closer to me and let the warmth of the fire heat my face.

With a sideways glance at Lola, I turned my eyes to Aaron and said, "Lola said something earlier that sort of made sense to me."

He gave me an odd look and waited.

I mentioned the party boats that tether together, and how the mob might be considering holding their big reunion out on the ocean so they wouldn't be as apt to be overheard by the FBI. "Is that possible? Can the FBI still listen in on their conversations if they are out on open water, rather than in port?"

He gave me a long look, shrugged and said he wasn't sure.

I laughed. "Now who's lying?"

Her eyes wide, Lola tossed another piece of wood onto the flames.

"You two have been hard at work figuring out what's going on. I guess it would be foolish of me to ask that you stop doing that before you find yourselves in trouble."

"I have no idea what you're talking about. It was simply a conversation we had earlier. I have enough to deal with in the form of Dave Martin without having the mob enter the equation. No thanks," I said with a snort.

"Keep it that way, Vin. Stay out of FBI things you know nothing about."

I opened my mouth and he shook his head. "Don't bother to deny that you aren't curious, or that you wouldn't get involved if the chance came along, I know better than that. Stay out of this mess until I bring you into it. Plans are being made, the danger is real, and if you didn't learn anything about the mob the last time you fell victim to them, then there's no hope for you at all. I'll guide you two through this, just pay attention to what I tell you, and hopefully we'll come through with flying colors."

"You're sure you want us along for the ride, then?" Lola asked.

"I do."

"Then we'll follow your lead, won't we Vinnie?"

"Sure thing," I said with the knowledge that nothing ever goes as planned. My life had never gone that way, so why would this? I think my life followed Murphy's Law. What could go wrong, always did.

Aaron rose from his chair and said goodnight. We watched him walk away and then settled back as Marcus arrived.

Lola leaned forward, tossed a piece of wood on the fire and murmured, "What do you think Marcus wants?"

"Only he knows."

He took the seat Aaron had vacated and lazily stretched out his legs. We waited a while until I couldn't stand the silence.

"What brings you by, Marcus?"

"There have been rumblings about mob-related affairs that I wanted to talk about. I know you and Lola have been on Johnny Pacci's yacht, that Aaron is not a happy camper, and by now he's probably been ordered to infiltrate whatever the mob has planned."

"And?" I asked.

"What part do you two play in this?"

"We aren't playing any part, why would you think so?"

With a glance at Lola, who had remained silent, he raised a brow and looked at me and remarked, "Please don't give me that line of crap, Lavinia."

Okay, so the only time Marcus referred to me as Lavinia was when I was in trouble for something or other to do with the mob and not minding my own business. Good golly. Surely he wouldn't lecture me? We'd nearly gone our separate ways partly because he thought I was reckless and partly because his bosses had pressured him about my activities. I refused to fall into old ways now, and simply gawked at him.

He sighed, and from the light thrown off by the flames, I could see his expression was serious.

"I'll say it again, don't get involved with the mob. You'll be outnumbered this time, more so than in the past. Neither of you should be placed in danger due to your inability to mind your business. I'm sure your father would wholeheartedly agree with me."

"I've had nothing to do with what's happened on this island other than having the misfortune of finding those two dead men. I didn't know either man, was unaware of their mob connections, and furthermore, I'm here on vacation with Lola."

He gave a snort of disbelief, I drew a breath, and Lola leaned forward.

"There's no reason to argue over something that doesn't concern Vinnie and me. If you're worried about us, we thank you for that. But, we don't need you to feel that way. I'm grateful you want to watch over us, Marcus, and Vinnie is, too. I'm sure of it. For all we care, the mobsters vacationing on Block Island can do whatever they want to one another, as long as they leave us alone. Was there anything else you wanted to discuss?"

He shook his head and stood up. "I can see I've wasted my time. It's clear that you two will do whatever you want, no matter how dangerous it becomes."

I rose, moved in close, and looked him in the eyes. "Thanks for coming by."

I stepped past him, tightened the afghan around my shoulders a bit more and marched toward the house. Was he really concerned or hoping to keep us from involvement with the mob? In the dark, I mimicked his words. "*I can see I've wasted my time.*" That was when I tripped and fell flat on my face just as my inner voice nagged me. *You should listen to him, Marcus knows what's going on and only wants you to be safe.* I rose from the ground and muttered, "Oh, will you shut up."

From inside the house, I heard the motorcycle leave, and blew a sigh of relief. Thank goodness, he was gone. The downstairs door closed softly, and light footfalls sounded on the stairs before Lola popped into my room. She sat on the bottom edge of my bed and gazed at me slumped against pillows propped up at the head of it.

"You two are as flammable as gasoline and a match these days. It's sad to see."

"I know. Sometimes he can be so judgmental, it makes me want to scream. Honestly, it does."

"He still loves you, Vin, you know that, don't you?"

"No, actually, I don't. People in love should be more understanding, accepting, and caring. All I get from him are judgments of my actions, tirades over minding my own business, and I never quite measure up to his standards. I know he was concerned for me whenever I was in danger, but he's constantly worried about how my actions impact his career. He's made it clear, over and over." I wiped tears that had sprung up and rolled down my cheeks.

She reached a hand out and rubbed the top of mine. "You aren't completely over him, are you?"

I shook my head and said, "Guess not, though when I see him around other women, it doesn't bother me like I thought it might. I believe parting ways was best for us. I can't, and won't, live with someone who thinks I'm a catastrophe waiting to happen." I snickered a bit. "Even if it's true."

Her light laughter raised my spirits, as it always did. "What was all that crap from Aaron tonight? Do you think he's sorry he asked us to help him with the investigation?"

"Who knows? I wonder why Aaron was on a rant. It could simply be he's worried over what can happen, but figures if he includes us he'll be able to keep things under control. We'll walk a fine line with the mob. You and I both know it. We'll have to be very cautious and turn a blind eye should unfortunate things happen."

"Unfortunate how?"

"I'm not sure. I would certainly hope no one would be murdered in front of us, or while we were on board a yacht. As I always say, we'll wing it. I do believe Aaron won't be far away from us if he can help it."

I leaned my head against the pillows and wished I was anywhere other than in this situation. There might be no one to help us if the mobsters turned on one another in our presence.

# Chapter 11

Rain pelted the windows as I arose from bed and swept the curtain aside to peer out the window. Hoping the entire day wouldn't be dreary, I straightened the room, made the bed, got dressed, and went downstairs for a cup of coffee. I could smell the marvelous aroma of it from the hallway and my mouth watered for the fresh brew.

Two mugs sat next to the coffee maker, and unwilling to wait for it to finish perking, I poured a half cup into the mug and added milk. Lola walked into the room. "Just couldn't wait, could you?"

I shook my head and looked up as the wind splattered raindrops against the kitchen window. "Nasty day. What are your plans?"

Pouring her own cup of brew, Lola said, "I'm not sure, my mother and Nana aren't up yet. I did think you and I might talk about how we can help Aaron, though."

We took our coffee into the sunroom and settled in. "What do you think he has in mind?"

Lola shook her head as her brows hiked a notch. "Who knows? One minute, he's determined to have our help, and the next he's putting on the brakes for fear he won't be able to rescue us if need be. Gosh, doesn't he know we—or at least, you—are capable?"

"I wouldn't go that far. After all, I was kidnapped not so long ago, and that scared the bejeepers out of me. If Frankie Tomatoes hadn't told those thugs not to hurt me, I don't know what would have happened. I had a few bad nights after that fiasco was over."

Her eyes widened as she stared at me. "You never let on, or I would have stayed at your house to help you through that."

I brushed her words away. "No need, it was something I had to work through on my own. Aaron doesn't know, and I'd rather it stayed that way."

"Sure, no problem. Aaron would have been alarmed over it anyway. In my opinion, men don't do well with that sort of thing. They're at a complete loss when it comes to women's emotions."

In an effort to change the subject, I said, "Are you and your mother going to meet your mob father, or what?"

"We haven't made a definite plan, though I believe she wants to see him while she's here. I'm unsure if I'll be invited along or not."

I glanced at the arched doorway of the room, leaned forward and whispered, "We could follow her when she sets out to meet with him. That way, you'll know who he is and can take things from there."

A smirk on her face, Lola leaned toward me and whispered, "I had the same thought."

A voice echoed from the kitchen, "What are you two whispering about in there?"

Eve poked her head around the edge of the doorway and stared at us with a look of curiosity.

I smiled, said good morning, and explained we were trying to be quiet until she and Nana had come downstairs.

Eve hesitated a moment before she nodded her head in acceptance of my answer. I rose, refilled my coffee cup and pulled the toaster from the cupboard. There's nothing quite like the smell of toasted bread. It makes my mouth water, but then, most food does. I guess I'm nothing but a foodie, and that's putting it mildly.

"I'll have toast, too, since you're making some," Lola said as she pulled a plate from the sideboard.

I filled the plate from the four-slot toaster. Lola fried eggs, ham, and cubed potatoes in a large skillet. Eve set the table and before long, we had a full-blown breakfast ready just as Nana came downstairs and Aaron drove into the yard.

Her laughter soft, Eve said, "He certainly has perfect timing."

We were still chuckling when Aaron rushed into the house and hung his rain jacket on a hook in the entry. "Pretty wet out there."

"Come on in and have breakfast, you'll feel better about the weather and everything else," Nana said beckoning him toward the table.

A full carafe of coffee sat on a hot pad, the platter of food sat in the center of the table, and we ate in silence for a while until Aaron glanced up and looked at me.

"What do you have planned for today?"

"Nothing yet, why?"

"I'd like you to meet someone." Unlike his smile, Aaron's eyes held a serious gleam.

"Just me?"

" If Lola doesn't mind, yes," he said with a dip of his head.

I glanced at Lola, who nodded slightly, and I agreed to go with him. We finished breakfast, then squared away the kitchen and dirty dishes before I scurried upstairs to fetch my jacket. As I returned downstairs, I heard Eve and Lola discuss a trip to the local bookstore along with a couple of other stops. Nana said she'd enjoy going, leaving me relieved that I wasn't dropping everyone to head out to who knew where with Aaron. He certainly had more on his mind than a ride around the island, of that, I was certain.

We left the women behind, drove along slick roads, went around the bend, and nearly ran into Dave Martin. He slid the driver's side window down when he slowed to a stop next to Aaron's truck. At this level, the men were eye-to-eye with serious demeanors. My pulse raced when neither man immediately spoke.

"Would you mind following me, Mr. Grant?"

"Sure, I'll turn around and be right along."

I leaned into the seat, nervous as a cat, and wondered what we were in for next, but surprisingly enough, I remained silent.

Aaron turned the huge Yukon around in the limited space of the roadside as though it was a Cooper and followed Dave Martin's truck. He took a sudden right turn onto Center Road and drove slowly through the Island Cemetery. We'd reached the far end of the grounds when he stopped altogether, left his truck, and climbed into the backseat of Aaron's.

"Cripes, it's a lousy day," Martin exclaimed.

"You live on an island. You're bound to have more rain than the mainland has. What's going on?" Aaron said in a resigned tone.

"More yachts and a few smaller vessels arrived late last night into the early morning hours. I'd like to know what the FBI thinks of the situation. Are we being overrun with mobsters and thugs, or what?"

I'd sidled sideways in the seat to see Martin's face. He appeared worried, his frown having grown deeper when his brows puckered in the middle. Clearly, the man was out of his depth where the mob was concerned. I knew the feeling well.

Aaron glanced in the rearview mirror, turned slightly in the seat and said, "I have no idea what they think. I can only assume there's a meeting of the New England crime families. I won't speculate what it's about, but I can say that you aren't equipped to handle what could take place while they're here."

"Could one family be killing off members of another family?" Martin asked.

"It would seem that way. The two men you've come across could very well be part of a house-cleaning problem. Johnny Boy Pacci has connections to the two dead men, other than that, I'm unsure who would have reason to murder them."

"What is your relationship with the two men, Ms. Esposito?"

I heaved a sigh and looked Martin straight in the eye. "As I have said many times, I have never had any relationship with either man."

He stared into my eyes and said evenly, "You know, Ms. Esposito, I just don't believe you."

"You know what, Officer Martin? I really don't care whether you believe me or not. I'm never having this conversation with you again, and you'd better believe that." I turned in the seat, stared through the windshield, listening to the rain thunder on the roof of the truck.

My father was right when he'd uttered the warning about policemen. This man would like as not toss me in a jail cell, lock the door and throw away the key, rather than take one word I said as truth. The fact that I lied wasn't in question, not as far as I was concerned, anyway. I'd protect my father, no matter what.

A mist had settled over the grounds, tombstones tilted at odd angles, and an apparition beckoned me. I shivered, tucked my hands in my coat, and said, "This place is creepy in foggy, rainy weather. Spooky, really spooky." I couldn't take my eyes off Dembrotti as he appeared to move closer.

Aaron glanced at me, then stared out the windshield to see what I saw. When he obviously didn't find what I was staring at, he turned back to Martin, who had turned his attention from me to ask Aaron if he thought there'd be any other dead men floating around.

Aaron shrugged a shoulder. "There's a possibility the killing will come to an end if the meeting between the families goes well. You must remember, not one of these people trusts the other, the *soldatis* are cold and calculating, they do as they're told without question or qualms. These men are sociopaths, feel no remorse, and are extremely dangerous. One slip-up by anybody and you end up deader than dead, especially law enforcement. Keep that in mind, Martin, should you decide to take on the mob."

The thick, heavy tension inside the truck made me want to open a window and set some of it free. Martin was angry, Aaron was more forbidding than I'd ever seen him, and I was worried, more so than I'd ever been. The only reason I didn't lower the window was due to the fear that Dembrotti's ghost was real and he'd enter the truck. Some vacation.

The rain had let up, the skies started clearing and the silence inside the vehicle had deepened.

"If you need a hand, let me know, Grant. I want these despicable people off my island as soon as possible."

"I'll keep that in mind."

Martin left the truck, got into his own and drove away. I heaved a sigh, opened the window as sunshine broke through the clouds and the fog disappeared, as did Dembrotti. I sucked in clean, crisp, ocean air, knowing I truly couldn't wait to get home.

His hand on mine, I looked at Aaron and realized he was worried.

"You're anxious to leave the island, aren't you?"

I nodded. "Now that Eve has arrived, it'll be more difficult than ever to steer clear of the mob. Lola's determined to do her thing, Eve has an agenda none of us are completely aware of, and I just want to go home. Never did I think I'd find myself in a mess such as this one, especially when I agreed to accompany Lola to Block Island. Good grief, it's a virtual nightmare."

He grinned, gave me an odd look, and said, "You usually relish this sort of challenge, why not this time around?"

Sidestepping is an art all its own. I'd been fairly good at it until Aaron entered my life. The man had all-seeing-eyes, he honed in on me like no other ever had, and frankly, it rattled me a tad more than I liked to admit.

I tried to sidestep and fervently wished it would work. It's disappointing to be wrong so often. "I merely thought I'd have a vacation without the mob, without any problems, and that I'd be able to help Lola deal with her identity crisis."

"I understand all that. Is there anything else you'd like to tell me?"

"Like what?"

"Normally, you'd embrace a chance to get the best of the mob, to bring justice for your two mob friends that were killed. I sense you're holding out on me, and that's not acceptable. We both know there's another reason for wanting to escape the island and what could possibly happen out here."

"I don't have one, I really don't, Aaron. One thing for certain is the idea that no matter where I go, the mob seems to be close by. It's getting old, really old."

He opened the truck door, got out, and I followed suit. We walked the graveyard, the quietness of the area cleared the cobwebs from my mind, the fear of Dembrotti's spirit lingering nearby began to dissipate, and Aaron murmured softly, "Do you trust me?"

I hesitated, and then stopped to look up into his dark eyes. "Why would you ask that?"

"It occurred to me that you are holding back because you don't trust me."

"I trust you, no question there."

"You're sure?"

"Why wouldn't I?"

"Because I'm an FBI agent."

I face him squarely. "Look, you have a job to do, I get that. I have a family to protect, I'm sure you realize it. If I don't trust you completely, it's due to that alone and nothing else. I value your friendship, I know you have my best interests in mind, and I appreciate that about you."

"So why won't you tell me what's bothering you, then? Does it have anything to do with your family?"

I blew a hefty sigh, brushed my hair away from my face as the wind whipped past, and muttered, "Whatever." My inner nag tormented me at the worst of times, and it did so now. *Be honest, you know he can deal with it. Tell him.*

"Fine."

His eyes widened a bit as he looked at me.

"After I was kidnapped by Frankie Tomatoes' goons, I had some tough nights, frightening nightmares, if you will. They only lasted a short time, but left me feeling vulnerable and fearful. Both of those things are new to me. Until then, I never walked around scared, but it doesn't take much for those emotions to pop up these days."

He stood still, not flicking an eyelash, not moving a muscle. I waited, afraid he'd think I'd had a breakdown of sorts or that I was lying. Who knew, maybe I had lost my marbles. He stepped close, drew me into his arms and held me tight. "You should have told me, I'd have been there for you. I won't let anything happen to you if I can prevent it, Vin. You believe that, don't you?"

Against his shoulder, I nodded. His scent filled my nostrils and I relaxed against him. He pulled back, locked lips with me. The moment fled and before I knew it, Aaron stepped back and stared into my face and said, "Sounds like a bad case of nerves. Eventually, you'll overcome those feelings. Just take one day at a time."

I nodded. "I'm trying. I'd like a break from the mob, is all."

"Good, now let's talk strategy for taking down those who have killed the two men you found."

So much for overcoming my feelings by using time to heal from the torment. Duh. I slid a sideways glance at him as I turned back toward the truck and wondered if I was brave enough to reach out to Dembrotti's ghost, if he could help me bring his killer to justice. I owed the man.

"I figured you'd have a plan of sorts, so let's discuss it."

"The families are aware of all that goes on, on the water and on land. They are wary of one another, and of strangers. Many of these thugs know who you are, who your father is, and now they know who Lola is. I had hoped she'd be willing to stay out of what's coming. It doesn't look like she'll stand aside and let the me do my job. I just don't want her to stumble into a situation she can't deal with. Why is her mother here?"

"She came at Lola's bidding. Lola wanted to face her down about her parentage, and Martin ordered us not to leave the island. Do you know who Lola's father really is?"

He opened his mouth, my phone rang, and the moment was lost. I answered to find a worried Lola on the line.

Her voice frantic, she spoke fast, and I listened carefully. "Where are you? My mother has some crazy idea of meeting up with my father and revealing his crimes to the FBI. Can you come back to the house? And, uh, leave Aaron out of this, okay?"

"I'll be right there. We'll work this out together, all right?"

"Just get back here, Vin."

The line went dead. I gawked at the phone for a second and then turned to Aaron, who waited for an explanation.

"Can our talk wait a while? I have to be the referee between Lola and her mother."

He nodded and murmured, "Don't want to be you."

I laughed, said it wouldn't be a first for me to become enmeshed in an Italian family squabble, and strode toward the SUV.

"You're sure that's all it is, then?"

"As far as I know. Lola is distraught and I need to get back."

"I have things to do, so I'll drop you off. What's with Lola's new personality?"

I grinned and said, "Since Lola has developed more backbone, she and her mother can't agree on much since the truth has come out. I'm uncertain whether Nana can handle an all-out war between the two of them."

"I have a few details to work out with Marcus and his partner. We'll talk later this afternoon, if you're free."

"That'll be fine." I rode to the house in silence, unwilling to talk for fear I'd blurt out more than I wanted Aaron to know. It would be better to find out Eve's great plan before I dumped that information on Aaron and screwed up what he had on his mob agenda.

He dropped me off at the door with a promise to call later and set a time to get together. I nodded, hurried into the house and found Eve and Lola sitting at the table. Neither woman uttered a word. They sat and fumed like nothing I'd ever seen. Lola's dark eyes snapped with anger. Her mother was tense, wound tight as a coiled spring.

I dropped into a chair and said, "What's going on?"

"Tell my mother how dangerous the mob is, Vinnie. Tell them about your abduction, the way you've been threatened, the awful things that have happened to you for getting too close to their business."

Eve gave Lola a frank stare and said, "Don't be dramatic."

"She's not being dramatic, Eve. She's telling you the truth. I was abducted by Frankie Tomatoes' men and held in the basement of a house in Federal Hill. It was by pure luck and ingenuity that I managed to get help before it was too late for me. In another instance, I was threatened by the mob for interfering with their money-laundering scheme. I could go on, but you get the point, I'm sure. I don't know what you're thinking, but playing in the mob's sandbox is pretty tricky and not for those with no experience."

"I don't think I like your tone," Eve said.

"I don't care what you like or don't like, Eve, I'm telling you this because your daughter is my best friend, she's been lied to all these years, and has asked for my help. Now what is it that you want to do?"

Her glare lightened and Eve glanced at Lola before bringing her eyes back to mine. "It was never my intention to hurt my daughter. I simply didn't want her life tainted by a gangster, and all that goes with that. I didn't lie, per se, I just avoided telling her about her lineage. I will say this much, though, she has her father's backbone."

"Tell us, Mom, just tell us who he is and why you want to get involved with him now," Lola asked in a low tone.

"He's no good. He was back then, too, I was young and stupid to not see it. Your father was the best thing to happen to me, I should have realized as much, instead of feeling lonely and vulnerable." Eve shook her head. "That's in the past, and best left there. What's important now is that he should no longer be able to hurt others, and I want to stop him before he does."

I sat quietly in my chair for a few seconds. "How?"

"He has done terrible things, bragged about them, even. I could tell the FBI and they could arrest him."

With a shake of my head, I said, "That's unlikely. The FBI has watched many of the families for years without being able to bring them to justice for their crimes. They don't take hearsay as truth, and they aren't likely to pay any mind to what you say. They deal in hard facts."

Eve listened to what I said, visibly shrank in her seat, and then began to cry. "Please don't get involved with these people, Lola. Nothing good can come of it."

Her eyes round and wide, Lola blanched as her mother came unglued. She reached out to her, took Eve's hand in hers and said, "Okay, I won't. If it means so much to you, then I'll steer clear of them all, Mom."

A tremulous smile met Lola's words. I left the two of them alone. I walked along the country lane and came to the tilted labyrinth signpost. Cautiously, I climbed the rickety steps and walked onto the grounds.

# Chapter 12

The labyrinth calmed me, though my mind never stopped spinning with all and everything that had happened in the past few days. Would, or could, I find the kind of peace I needed? I wondered aloud and then smiled at the absurdity of the question.

The overhead sun was high, brought sweat to my brow, and I turned to walk up the hill to sit on the bench under the trees and overhanging foliage. I had started to relax, and wiped the sweat from my face when cool air settled over me.

*"I been tryin' to reach you, Lavinia."*

Startled, I jumped and clung to the arm of the bench as I slid my gaze slowly to the right. Dembrotti sat next to me, his spirit was nearly solid, and I began to shake.

*"You didn't believe I was tryin' to contact you, did you?"*

Speechless, I shook my head. My heart pounded so loudly, I thought I could hear it.

*"Johnny did me and Conigliaro in. He's your man, Lavinia."*

"W-why?" I stammered.

*"He thought we turned federal on him. No way we would do that, Lavinia, no way."*

I glanced around, realized I was talking to a ghost, and furthermore, heard him talk back. "Who gave him that idea?"

*"Jimmy Byrne, the Irish mobster from South Boston."*

"Hey, Vinnie? Are you up there?"

I heard Lola's voice, and saw her red hair bobbing up over the top of the steps. I slid a glance sideways and found I was alone. Dembrotti was gone. I blew out a sigh of relief, worried over what had just happened, and wondered if I had imagined it all.

"There you are," she said with a smile. "I haven't been to this labyrinth in years. Have you walked it already?"

I rose and walked down to meet Lola at the edge of the path. "I came here with Marcus a couple days ago. It was so peaceful, that I thought I might try it again."

Lola made her way through the narrow path, and joined me on the bench. I watched her and considered how much she resembled Jimmy Byrne. Her curly auburn locks, freckled face, sweet smile, all reminded me of the photo I'd seen of Byrne while doing research online.

Lola gave me a puzzled stare. "You're lost in thought, what's going on?"

"Nothing. How's your mother?"

"She's going back to the mainland, is giving up her mad idea to call the FBI, and I have you to thank for that. She can be quite naive at times. I think she wanted to punish my *real* father for their tryst and her pregnancy. I can't blame her there, but hey, it does take two, right?"

I glanced at her in surprise and then started to laugh. "You're right. On a different subject, do you believe in ghosts?"

"What?"

"Ghosts, do you believe in them?"

"I've never given it much thought, why?"

I'd caught her interest and now her focus was trained on me. Oh, boy.

I shrugged. "Just wondering."

"Don't give me that line of crap, you wouldn't have asked if there wasn't something behind the question. Have you seen a ghost?"

Unwilling to shy away from the question, I blurted, "I think Dembrotti is trying to reach out to me."

Her mouth hung open for a second as she gasped at the idea. Then she said, "When did this happen?"

"I thought I saw him beckoning me a couple of times—scared me half to death, too. When I came here today, he appeared next to me, right where you're sitting now."

Lola leapt off the seat, jumped around a bit, and scanned the entire area.

"Sit down. He left when you called to me from the steps."

"You're sure he was here, though, right? It wasn't your imagination at play?"

"I think he was here. He said he'd been trying to reach me. He also said Johnny Pacci had him and Conigliaro killed."

"Why?"

"Johnny thought they had turned to the feds and given him up."

"How did Johnny learn that?"

I turned my eyes toward the labyrinth, said a silent prayer for forgiveness, and lied for all I was worth. "He didn't get that far. You arrived and scared him away."

"So, you think Johnny had them killed, then? Without any proof?"

"Lola, how would a ghost give me proof? I can't even believe I told you about it, I can hardly come to terms with the idea myself."

Her body relaxed as she eased against the back of the bench. Lola smiled and said, "You have the best experiences."

"Says the person who hasn't had to live through them," I said. "Let's walk into town and have a beer, shall we?"

"Good idea, enough of ghosts, mobsters, and murder. I could use a break from all of it. How do you manage such a constant barrage of this stuff? It's overwhelming, especially the dead body thing."

Lola and I walked down the hill, took the rickety, scary stairs to the road and walked into town. We'd bought our beer, sat on the stone wall overlooking the bay and listened to the gulls as they cried and swayed in the wind. How freeing it must be to drift on something you couldn't see, that held you up and allowed you to float in the air. Lost in thought, I was startled when Marcus climbed onto the wall and sat next to me.

"You look like you're a long way from here, Vin."

"Just admiring the gulls," I admitted.

He leaned forward to see Lola. "Are you two taking a break from the mob?"

"We are," I said.

"Glad to hear it. They've arrived in numbers, their yachts are unbelievable. Guess there's more money in crime than I ever imagined," Marcus noted as he pointed to several yachts floating offshore.

"Those are beautiful, aren't they?" Lola remarked as she held her hand over her brow to block the sun while she stared at the crafts.

"There are two Delfinos, one bigger than the other," I said.

Marcus grinned. "I didn't know you were a boat connoisseur."

I laughed. "I'm not. I saw one in a magazine and then those two. That's about all I know about boats, yachts, or whatever they're called."

"You went out with Johnny Pacci though, right?"

"We did. His yacht is gorgeous, and he told me Lanky Larry did the decor for him. Has two of Larry's paintings as well. It was an interesting encounter, but not one we'd care to repeat, do we, Lola?"

She shook her head and offered Marcus the Julia smile. He responded as most men do, by becoming putty in her hands. Dang, I wish I could manage that response.

"I'm off duty tonight, why don't you two meet me for dinner at Ballard's Inn?"

Before I could refuse, Lola said, "We'd love that, Marcus. What time?"

I gave her a look. She smiled and then agreed when he said we should meet at seven o'clock. He left us sitting there.

"Be a good sport, Vinnie. It's not every day we both get invited to dinner by such a handsome man."

I arched a brow and gave her a look of disbelief. "You'd better not be up to anything devious, Lola. Let's go to Nana's and see your mother off home."

We hiked the distance and met Lola's mother on the stairs as she brought her luggage down. I took it from her and stowed it in the

backseat of Lola's car. Nana wished Eve goodbye and we walked her to
the car.

Lola drove away with her mother chatting as they went. I folded
my arms and smiled as the car disappeared down the road. Nana said,
"I don't know about you, but I could use a glass of wine."

I laughed outright, followed her inside and poured us each a goblet
of Chardonnay. We took them onto the dock, settled into chairs in the
sun, and toasted ourselves by clinking the glasses against one another.

"Do you think they have gotten their issues straightened out,
Nana?"

"It looks like a good start. Eve can be difficult, but Lola is a lovely,
warm and forgiving young woman. It was disturbing to see her in such
a state."

"Me, too. Especially when I didn't know what the problem was."

"You know who her gangster father is, don't you, Vinnie?"

I shook my head. "Not for certain, and until I do, I won't venture a
guess. Please don't ask me."

"Okay, I won't," Nana said and sipped her wine.

It wasn't long before Lola drove into the yard and parked the
Cooper. She scooted inside and came out carrying a wine glass and the
Chardonnay with her.

"Whew, glad that's over. Mom's on her way home, I even waited for
the ferry to leave in order to make sure she didn't change her mind."

Her sense of humor restored, the old Lola was back, for the
moment, anyway. The remainder of our stay might be a different matter
altogether.

With a smile, Nana said, "You appear relieved to have discussed the
situation with your mother."

"I am, believe me, that was long overdue, and I'm really glad it's
over with. You know how she can be."

Nana gave a brief nod, said she was going to the church supper and
then staying for Bingo, so we needn't worry about dinner where she

was concerned. She rose from the chair, empty wine glass in hand, and walked toward the house. I watched her and wondered what life on the island had been like for her all these years. There was no doubt that she was an islander, she rarely took the ferry to the mainland, saying it was too noisy and busy for her liking.

"Did your mother offer any advice before she boarded the ferry?"

Lola snickered and said Eve had rambled on about steering clear of the mob and possibly finding a nice man like Aaron Grant to marry and settle down with."

I gave a hoot of laughter. "Yeah, well, she has no idea who and what he is, does she? Anyone married to that man would worry about him getting murdered or flipping to the other side, rather than staying a lawman. No thank you."

"So, if Aaron wanted to get serious, you would reject him?"

I twirled the remaining wine in my glass while I pondered her question.

"Well?"

I took a breath and said, "Not that he isn't handsome, and we have a good relationship, but I fear he'd try to change me. He'd likely want more than I'm willing to give at this moment. Don't get me wrong, he's wish-list material, for sure, but after the break with Marcus, I've considered not dating a lawman of any kind, not even a security guard."

Lola shook her head. "You can't expect me to believe you wouldn't jump at the chance to get down and dirty with him?"

"Yep, that covers it. He's a tempting morsel, but there's baggage that goes with it and I don't want that."

"You have never had involvement issues, Vin. Why now?"

"Marcus broke my heart, and I know I broke his. A life with him might never have worked out well for either of us. We both knew it, but old habits die hard. If you're thinking of playing matchmaker tonight, please don't."

Lola crossed her heart with two fingers. "I promise, I won't.

"Thanks, now what are we wearing to dinner? My choices are limited since I had no idea we'd stay for more than a few days or a week and be invited besides."

"Come on, let's go see what Wild Flowers Boutique carries that you might like." Fired up over clothes shopping, Lola scrambled from the chair, and we hurried off to stroll Water Street.

We browsed the boutique, found a super dress that fit me like a second skin, and left it with the clerk while Lola looked for the perfect outfit. I took the time to choose jewelry while she tried on clothes. I gave her my opinion when she called me to the dressing room.

When she swung the door open, I gazed at the burnt orange and golden yellow top with a matching skirt. The tie-dye effect was stunning, the outfit was perfect for her. "That is gorgeous, you should buy it. Those colors set off your hair and compliment your complexion."

Her excitement was palpable as she whipped the door closed and changed back into her Capri pants and jersey.

We made our purchases, then walked on down the street in search of ice cream and ended up at The Ice Cream Place. We indulged in sundaes topped with sprinkles and sat outside under an umbrella table to watch tourists wander past.

Lola glanced at her watch. "We have time to take a ride around the island, are you game?"

"Sure, why not. We aren't meeting Marcus until later."

Driving from one end of the island to the other, we stopped frequently to enjoy breathtaking views along the way. I felt freer than I had in a while, and figured Lola must be experiencing the same. Her laughter and spirit were light as we went from one place to another.

We reached Mohegan's Bluffs and took the short trail from the parking lot down onto a multitude of steps that led to the beach. Going down was the easy part, climbing the stairs would be a challenge for the hardiest. I lost count as we descended and left off at one hundred and forty steps. There were handrails and drawn out places to stop on the way to and from the beach.

There weren't any beach goers, and I wondered if they hadn't yet had the opportunity to discover the place. It was glorious, the views spectacular and I wished I'd brought my swimsuit. My happiness over the spot was brief when I rounded a curve in the beach. Rocks covered with seaweed, also harbored an arm that protruded above a larger rock. I froze mid-stride, backed away, and told Lola to call the police.

Her smile dimmed, her eyes rounded, and she did as I asked as she glanced past me. "What do you want them to come here for?"

I raised my arm and pointed. "I think a body has washed ashore over there. I can see an arm protruding from the edge of that flat boulder and I don't want to look."

Nodding, she said, "Vin, you'd better look. What if you're mistaken and you get Martin out here? He already dislikes you."

*Gee thanks, I didn't know that.* My inner voice kicked in and I tried to drown out the harping that always told me what I should be doing by saying, "Okay, Lola, you stay right there."

I edged closer, holding onto the notion that maybe my imagination was working overtime. When I arrived at the rock and peered over it, I knew I'd been foolish to hope I was mistaken. The body was badly battered, apparently the tide had driven it against the rocks before it became stuck. His dark hair held a bit of gray at the temples, and I shuddered when I realized I was staring down at Johnny Boy Pacci. His shirt no longer white, his tie was entwined with the rope secured around his neck. Thank goodness there was no blood.

"It's a dead man. You better call, right now, Lola."

# Chapter 13

Sirens whined and then stopped. Trucks drew to a halt, and I watched with a hand shading my eyes, as Martin descended followed by a crew of rescuers. This time, they came prepared by carrying the basket stretcher to load the body into and bring it upward. I didn't envy these men. The trek up with a body would be a struggle. Dead weight is heavy. Luckily, Johnny Pacci wasn't a large man, just a dead one.

When the entire ensemble stood not five feet from me, Martin told them to stay where they were and approached me alone. The gleam in his eyes was cold, his expression tense and I knew I'd be in for a rough time.

"When did you find him?" Martin asked as he peered at the body.

"Just before we called you."

"Do you know this man?"

"He's John Pacci."

"How do you know?"

"I met him at a party the other night."

"Wasn't this the guy you and Lola went out on the water with?"

He looked up when I didn't answer. I nodded and then looked away to see Lola gawking from a distance.

"You won't get off easy this time, Ms. Esposito."

"I think I'll call my lawyer now," I said and walked away. I slid the phone from my pocket and hit speed dial for my father's number. He answered on the first ring.

"What's the matter?"

"I just found Johnny Pacci dead on the beach. He died the same way as the others, and Dad, I know he killed Dembrotti and Conigliaro. He thought they'd turned to the feds and gave him up."

"Don't say another word, I'll call an attorney and he'll be with you soon. Say nothing, you hear me?"

"Got it. Hurry though, will you?"

The line was dead. My father had hung up and was now probably ranting like a maniac about his only daughter not being able to mind her own business. As long as he called an attorney, he could rant and rave all he wanted. A feeling of desperation began to take hold as I reached Lola's side.

"It's Johnny Pacci," I whispered. "My father is sending an attorney over. We aren't to utter a word, understand? Not one word. Dad's really upset."

She stared off into the horizon and then shook her head. "It was inevitable that you'd find one more body, Vin. Only you would have that misfortune." With that said, Lola turned and started across the beach toward the steps. Her feet shuffled small clouds of sand as she marched away, her back stiff, and her attitude one of acceptance.

"Where's Lola going?" Martin asked.

"We are going to Nana's house, you can question us there." I gave him a glance and followed Lola's lead. I couldn't get off the beach fast enough, the day was ruined, and dinner with Marcus was likely to be miserable. Great. I'd just spent money on a nice outfit, too. Crap.

I climbed and climbed until I thought I'd never reach the top of the steps. When I came abreast of the road, I found Lola leaning against her car, her arms folded and her face to the sun.

"You made it. I wasn't sure I would," I remarked.

"It is a tough climb, but worth it. The views are gorgeous, aren't they?" Lola asked.

"Let's get back to Nana's, shall we? I told Martin he could question us there if he needs to."

With a grimace, Lola muttered, "Perfect."

"I'm really sorry, Lola, honestly, I am."

"You had nothing to do with Johnny's death, Vin. Don't apologize, it wasn't your fault he grew up to be a mobster and do nasty and dishonest things in his life. It was inevitable he'd end up this way."

We got into the car and cruised the roads at a slow pace, as though she didn't want to arrive at her grandmother's house too soon. It occurred to me that she might be hoping Nana would have left for the church supper, but didn't say as much.

As she pulled onto the side of the road where many people stopped at this vantage point, I turned in the seat to look at her.

"I have to tell you something. You'll think I've lost my mind, but rest assured, I haven't. Dembrotti's ghost told me Johnny Pacci had him and Conigliaro killed. They were both murdered in the same way and now Johnny has suffered the very same death."

"Are you nuts? You actually spoke with Dembrotti's ghost? You didn't tell me that part," Lola yelled.

"Not in the least and yes, we spoke."

"Good lord, you had a conversation with a ghost. I can't believe it."

"Me either, but there you have it. He sat next to me and said he and his buddy had been killed by Johnny because he thought they'd turned to the feds and offered him up."

"Did they?" Lola asked.

"Not a chance. Dembrotti was too smart for that. How he managed to end up dead is a mystery. He was a huge brute, as was Conigliaro. Ham hocks for hands, beefy bodies, tall, and dangerous. They'd been around for years, and knew how to stay alive, until now."

"So, how do you think they ended up dead if they were so smart?"

"I haven't a clue. You?"

Lola shook her head.

My phone jingled and I looked at the screen. "It's Aaron."

"You might as well answer the call, otherwise he'll hunt us down."

I tapped the screen and said, "Hello?"

"Tell me you didn't find Johnny's body?" Aaron demanded.

"I can't lie to you, I found it. As a matter of fact, Lola and I found it."

"Christ almighty, Lavinia, I suppose you've called Martin?"

"Of course, it's not my job to take care of the bodies. It's his."

"You should have called me first."

I held the phone away, glared at it, then put it back to my ear and asked, "Why would I do that?"

"It's complicated. Where are you right now?"

"Not far from Nana's."

"Fine, I'll meet you there. Marcus will be with me, too."

The call ended. I tucked the phone into my pocket and said, "Aaron and Marcus are meeting us at Nana's. We'd better get going."

"Vin, are you scared?"

I looked at her and then said, "Oh, yeah."

"Me, too." Lola started the car and we rolled onto the country lane. We rounded the bend and took a right into Nana's yard. The house was closed, and apparently Nana was gone since the front door and windows were closed tight. A definite sign nobody was home. Nana enjoyed the ocean breeze, and usually kept a few windows open, as well as the front door.

We'd gotten out of the car and were taking our shopping bags from the backseat when Aaron drove in. Marcus sat in the front seat next to him, and I could have sworn there was a look of concern of his face. I sighed and wondered if it was for me, Lola, or both of us.

They walked alongside us and entered the house right on our heels. I tossed my shopping bag on the staircase, as did Lola. "You two want coffee or a cold drink? I think there's iced tea in the fridge." Lola pointed to it.

Aaron shook his head. "Nothing, thanks. Just an explanation of what happened."

I made quick work of our find before I got up and brought the pitcher of iced tea to the table along with glasses for those who might want a beverage. I knew we could all use something a bit stronger, though it didn't lend to keeping our wits about us.

The refreshing taste of the tea calmed my angst and I glanced at Lola. She gave me a quick look and fiddled with her glass. The silence lasted so long I was afraid I'd utter something I would regret and simply leaned back in the chair and waited for either man to speak first.

"You didn't see anyone else on the beach?" Marcus asked.

"No one. Pacci had been there for quite some time by the look of him. Washed up and got snagged on the rock." I shivered and looked away from Marcus's intense gaze.

"You do have the worst luck, Vinnie," he said.

"I know, and it's getting old, real fast."

His elbows on the table, Aaron asked, "What were you doing on that part of the island?"

Lola leaned forward, set her glass aside, and said, "We had time before dinner, so we decided to visit some of the most breathtaking places on the island. Little did we know how our sightseeing would end."

"Indeed," Aaron remarked.

His earlier remark about calling him first had stuck in my mind and I needed to know what he'd meant. I asked, and saw him hesitate a second, before he said, "I would have liked to get a look at him first. He was supposedly at the bottom of Conigliaro and Dembrotti's deaths, so why would he end up the same way?"

"I don't know," I answered. The next question on the tip of my tongue was how he'd concluded that Pacci had ordered the other men's deaths. Before I could ask, Lola jumped in. We must have been on the same wavelength, because she asked that very question.

His eyes narrowed a tad before Aaron answered.

"I have information that led me to believe Pacci was behind the deaths."

Had he seen Dembrotti's ghost? I nearly snorted aloud at the idea and abruptly poured more tea into my half-empty glass. I raised the pitcher toward the others, who shook their heads, but stared at me.

In a soft voice, Marcus asked, "Do you want to share your thoughts?"

My inner voice piped up, always at the worst moment, and ranted, *"Don't tell them, they'll think you've finally lost your last marbles. Some things are better left unsaid."*

For once, I wholeheartedly agreed. I sighed and said that Aaron's information was correct.

His brows rose slightly, but Marcus didn't utter a word.

"They worked for Pacci, right? So if they were killed, common sense would indicate he was the one who gave the orders. At least, it seems that way to me."

Both men nodded and Aaron picked up where Marcus left off. "You wouldn't happen to have inside information, would you?"

I gave him a steady look. "Where would I get that?"

He glanced down and then back at me. "I think you know what I'm asking."

I did a slow burn that turned into a raging inferno of anger. One way or another, Marcus and Aaron always intimated at my father's possible involvement with the mob. Christ, couldn't they give me a break, just once in a while? "I have no idea what you're getting at. I haven't a clue as to why these people died, where that happened, or who did the deeds. Why don't you run along back to your information link and find your answers there?" Okay, so I was on a rant of my own.

"Vinnie, don't get upset. We all know your father has ties to the mob world, otherwise you would probably be dead by now. You've tread on so many dangerous toes in the past, it's a wonder you're still among the living," Aaron said.

I jumped from the chair, sent it over backwards and pointed toward the door. "Get out, just get out, and don't come back." I glared at Aaron and then shouted, "When you get to the mainland, move out of my house."

I stomped up the stairs, slammed the bedroom door, and started to cry. These latest episodes had worn me down so badly, I wondered if I could brace myself for another.

My cell phone jingled, my father was on the line. Crap.

I wiped my tears, quickly blew my nose, and answered the call.

"Hi, Dad, what's up?"

"Are you all right? You sound strange."

"I'm fine, why are you calling?" Please, no more bad news.

"The attorney is on his way, he just boarded the ferry. Remember, keep your own counsel, not a word to anyone. Understand? Cops are not your friend, Lavinia. If you never listened to me before, listen now." The line went dead and I flung the phone across the room as Lola walked in.

# Chapter 14

"I think I need some alone-time, why don't you meet Marcus for dinner and I'll stay here," I urged.

With a guilty smile, Lola admitted, "It might not be wise, I told them both off before they left. This constant badgering you about your father is ridiculous. Even if he was involved with the mob, why would you give him up? He's family for goodness sake. Doesn't anyone other than Italians understand that?"

"I know, huh?" I agreed.

"Aaron was shocked that you'd kick him out of his apartment. You should have seen his face as you left the room. It was priceless," Lola said with a snicker. "They certainly pushed the envelope too far this time."

"Indeed, they did. For what it's worth, I don't want him out of the apartment. I think he's only been staying to see if he can get to my father, or use him to get to the mob, but I'm comfortable knowing he's upstairs. If there's a connection between Dad and the mob, I don't care what it is. He's still my father, and I refuse to go against him. Even if he has a mere alliance, it's none of my business and I won't get involved."

The Julia smile in place, Lola said, "Smart thinking, Vin. Now, go take a shower, put on that cute dress you bought and let's go out to dinner on our own."

I nodded and headed for the bathroom.

On my way down the corridor Lola called after me, "I wouldn't want to waste the clothes we bought today."

We parked outside the Spring House Hotel on Spring Street and went inside, hoping we wouldn't have a long wait. As luck would have it, we'd arrived early enough to avoid the crowd, and got to sit on the patio to enjoy the ocean view while perusing the menu.

Sangria was the drink of the evening for both of us. I ordered Chicken Saltimbocca, while Lola ordered the Pork Chop Milanese dish. Both looked tasty and we waited with anticipation for delivery of dinner prepared by someone other than us.

Gulls drifted on wind currents and we watched them dive gracefully into pools of water below to retrieve their own fare. When the waiter arrived, we tucked into our exquisitely prepared dinners as though we hadn't eaten in a week. Frankly, it seemed that way and I put it down to the salt-laden, fresh air.

With dinner finished, we lounged on the patio until dark and then drove home. It had been a pleasant evening, no pressure, no talk of murder or gangsters, nothing but enjoying the scenery, eating good food, and drinking the best Sangria I'd ever tasted. Now if only the rest of my life would run as smoothly as tonight had.

We'd no sooner parked in front of Nana's house, when Dave Martin drove in and stopped next to us. I moaned. Lola rolled her eyes, and we got out of the Cooper to meet the man.

"Good evening, on your way to—or from—a party?" Martin asked.

"We went to dinner," Lola said and walked ahead of him toward the house. Nana was still out, and for that, I gave a sigh of relief. Who knew how she'd react when she found out about our afternoon misadventure.

We sat at the kitchen table as Lola pointed to a seat across from us. "You might as well sit down."

He nodded, gave us both a cool-eyed once over and said, "A while ago, a lawyer stopped at the station asking for you, Ms. Esposito. He said he's staying at Ballard's Inn. Mind my asking why you think you need an attorney?"

I shrugged. "Maybe I don't want to be railroaded by the police. After all, you don't like me, have offered to lock me up, and for no real reason other than the fact that I'm Italian. Let's just say I'm all about protecting myself from the likes of you."

His face stiffened, his glared intensified, and then he turned to Lola. "Will you be getting a lawyer, Ms. Trapezi?"

She remarked, "If I need one, Vinnie and I can share."

He took a deep breath, let it out, and shook his head. "I'm trying to solve three murders, keep an eye on the mob, and keep pace with the FBI. The island is loaded with tourists, and has citizens who have lived here for years, good people I want to protect from the likes of hoods, bums, and criminals. It's my first priority, and I can't do it alone. I need your assistance, which will allow me to keep the peace and maintain safety. Surely you understand that."

I said nothing. Lola took the opportunity to ask, "You want our help? In what way?"

I glanced at Martin and then stared at Lola. No way was I about to give up what I knew to this man, not now, not ever.

"Just tell me what you think is going on, and I'll take it from there. You both seem to know more than I do about these mobsters with their fancy boats and the thugs on them that are armed to the teeth."

Lola slid her gaze toward mine and I gave a slight nod.

"When we were invited onto John Pacci's boat, it was a social affair, nothing more. While we were on the bay, we noticed two men on the boat who appeared dangerous and were undoubtedly armed. Scary men, to say the least. Mr. Pacci was charming until he received a phone call. He ordered his henchman to give us whatever we needed, which probably meant the man should keep an eye on us, and then we came ashore. Mr. Pacci couldn't get rid of us fast enough. Other than that, we have nothing to share. We're as much in the dark as you are. Honestly."

"You have no idea who killed Pacci, or why?"

"I think someone's cleaning house. Pacci might have caused trouble for the wrong person and payback was the result," Lola said.

"What do you think, Ms. Esposito?"

"The same. Lola and I have no clue to what's taking place or why all this is happening, especially here."

He rose from his chair, pushed it back in place, and thanked us for being truthful. I didn't buy his act for a moment, but said nothing. He took his leave and we watched him go, relieved to see the back of him. How do I get into these messes?

I called my father, who gave me the attorney's name, and then called the hotel.

"Could you connect me to Mr. Casella's room?"

"Certainly, ma'am."

I heard a baritone voice say 'hello'.

"This is Vinnie Esposito, is this Mr. Casella?"

"Yes, it is. Your father sent me to advise you. Is everything all right, Ms. Esposito?"

"At the moment. If you would be so kind as to call me in the morning, we can meet."

"Certainly. Why don't we get together at nine here at the hotel?"

"See you then," I said and hung up.

Lola asked, "What time?"

"Nine, and he sounds as though he has some brains. Unlike the other lawyer my father got for me, who was playing on both teams at once. I'm exhausted. I think I'll turn in for the night."

"It's not windy outside, are you sure you don't want to sit by the fire pit and relax?" Lola asked hopefully.

I smiled and said, "Sure, why not. I'll change and meet you out there."

The moon and stars brightened the night as we sat by the fire pit chatting. A truck drove into the yard.

Nana hopped out and Aaron walked her to the door.

We heard their conversation as they went.

"Thank you so much for the ride. My friend left early and I wasn't looking forward to walking the dark road alone."

"No problem, Mrs. Trapezi, it was my pleasure," Aaron said and wished her goodnight.

A moment later, he strolled in our direction and said, "Vinnie, could we talk?"

"Do we have to?"

"I think it would be wise. Come on, I'll take you out for a drink and maybe we can clear the air."

I glanced at Lola, whose eyes were big and round as she nodded and whispered, "Go ahead."

"Fine," I murmured and left her sitting by the fire.

I climbed into the passenger seat of the Yukon and we drove to the Mohegan Cafe and Brewery on Water Street and settled in. Aaron ordered drinks without asking for my input and I let his presumptuousness pass without comment. He knew I liked wine, and that's what he ordered.

He reached across the table to take my hand, but I slid them under the table and stared at him. He drew back, looked mildly uncomfortable and then said, "I overstepped. I was out of line, and I'm sorry. I should never have said what I did about your father. There's no proof that he's involved with any of this, or those people, and I was wrong to say as much."

"And?"

"Do I have to move out?" His brown eyes were pleading and I couldn't resist them.

I snickered. "No, you don't have to move out. I was very angry and whatever came to mind flew out of my mouth." He was about to speak, when I continued, "That said, my family is *not* fair game for you or your crew." I was unwilling to say who Aaron was aligned with or worked for. Sometimes walls have ears, and one never knew who was listening.

"Good enough, I will remember that. I must say, though, you have the worst luck of anyone I've ever met. How do you manage to stay sane through it all?"

I laughed. "You think I'm sane? For a while there, I thought I'd lost my last marble." I crossed my heart, and then said, "Honestly, I did."

Our drinks arrived. I fiddled with the stem of the glass and wondered what had really brought him to see me tonight.

"Speaking of honesty, I would appreciate yours."

"I've been honest."

"Sure, you have." I pushed the glass aside and readied to leave the booth.

He grabbed my hand. "Wait, what do you think I've been dishonest about?"

I sat, sighed, rolled my eyes, and said, "Where to start? Oh, yeah, I know—why did you really move into my house?"

Hesitant, Aaron finally said, "Initially, you were a person of interest to my, uh, crew, but once I moved in, you became of personal interest to me."

"Meaning?"

"I believe we've become more than friends, don't you?"

"I guess. I like having you at the house, I feel more comfortable knowing you're upstairs."

"Nothing more?"

"Like what?"

"Romantically?"

"I don't think so, it's not a good idea. I had a relationship with Marcus and look where that ended? Repeating that mistake wouldn't be healthy for me."

Aaron leaned forward and murmured, "Because of my job?"

I nodded and drank my wine.

"That's what I thought. I've refrained from asking you due to that issue. I'd like nothing better than that, but I, too, feel we would be on dangerous ground. Both emotionally and otherwise."

We sat quietly for a while and then left the brewery. Aaron dropped me off at Nana's and I said good night. I went into the house and found Lola waiting anxiously for an update.

"Tell me, tell me," she insisted.

"He apologized, and asked if he really had to move out." Then I summed up the rest of the conversation.

"Wow, you two really got things out into the open. So, what's next?"

"We didn't get that far. We agreed my family is off limits and if I get so much as an inkling he has thrown that agreement aside, I will force him to move out."

She nodded and said goodnight. I waited until Lola's bedroom door closed before I tiptoed down the stairs and out the door. It had begun to grow cold, the wind had picked up, but I needed fresh air and headed toward the smoldering fire pit. I tossed a couple of logs onto the coals and hoped it would catch.

An afghan lay in a pile on the Adirondack chair closest to the pit and I huddled underneath it. Startled when I heard his voice, I sat up and turned toward Marcus who stood on the edge of the light cast from the low flames.

"You nearly scared me to death," I said and motioned to a chair across from me so I could see him.

"I thought I should check on you after today's situation. You sure were angry at Aaron. Does he plan to move out?"

"He doesn't want to and has apologized for his behavior. I'm not saying I trust that he won't continue to investigate my family, but if he knows what's good for him, he'll tread lightly."

Marcus grinned. "He sure got under your skin, I thought you were going to throw a punch or two when you flew into anger. I haven't seen you that angry in quite some time. Hit a sore spot, did he?"

"Are you really going to go there?" I asked and stared at him.

Marcus shrugged and sat back in the chair, his eyes on mine. "He won't give up, you know. Even though he finds you attractive, and would like to get close to you, be careful, Vinnie. He's FBI and that's worse than being a State Trooper. Law enforcement officers are dogs with a bone, but agents are purebred Pit Bulls, no matter what branch they work for. His undercover status makes him even more dangerous. Keep that in mind, okay?"

"I will. What's the mob doing here, anyway?"

"Damned if I know. It's the last thing this island needs. The local Leos aren't able to handle what could happen, there are only two of us from the state level and one FBI agent to deal with a slew of cold, deadly, criminals. I'll admit, I'm worried and I think Aaron is, too." Marcus looked at me for a long moment. "Is Lola all right after finding John Pacci today?"

"She never got a look at him, I made sure of that. She's developed more backbone, and I remember you calling her Little Miss Dynamite. You always knew she was braver than she looked, didn't you?"

He nodded and laughed. "Every now and then I'd see this spark in her eyes. I guess I was right."

"You certainly were. When she decided to challenge her mother by going out on Johnny's boat and then had a flat out argument with her over the mob, I was surprised and even asked if aliens had taken the real Lola." We both snickered over the thought.

"She'll be your ally if you get into a tight corner, Vin. I bet she's even told Dave Martin where to get off, hasn't she?"

"Indeed, more than once. He came by earlier tonight and wanted to play nice, be friends, asked for our help, even. Neither of us bought into that crap for one minute, but Lola dealt with him using her Julia Roberts smile and her innocence. He said a lawyer had stopped by looking for me and wanted to know why I was seeking legal counsel. I wasn't as sweet or charming as Little Miss Dynamite. That way he knows where we stand with one another."

"I heard there was a lawyer looking for you. Smart move, Vin. Martin isn't your friend and you'd be wise to listen to the attorney's advice."

I snuggled under the afghan and wondered how we had managed to have such a conversation. There'd been no recriminations, accusations, or snarky remarks from either of us toward the other.

"Martin doesn't like me, and I feel the same toward him. He's biased because I'm Italian and has the impression that all of us are related to the mob. Talk about small-minded. It's totally annoying, and it's all I can do not to lose my temper every time I see the man."

"Remember, things on an island are different than the mainland. Life here is isolated much of the year, and his department isn't prepared to take on the likes of what could become an instant war should one of the mobsters take exception to another."

At his words, my curiosity ratcheted up a notch. "What's up now?"

"There was an incident about an hour or so ago where one of the boats issued a distress call. They were sinking and had to be towed to shore before the boat went under. When Martin questioned the crew onboard the yacht, he got nowhere. He hit the code of silence and was quite angered by it. There will be repercussions over the incident, especially between the mobster who owned the boat and the suspected mobster who ordered the yacht to be sunk."

The fire had died down, I yawned and rose, taking the afghan with me. Marcus got up, walked alongside me, his arm slung around my shoulders, and whispered in my ear. "Stay as far away from the marina as you can, Vin. I wouldn't want you caught in the crossfire, okay?" He kissed me and walked toward the road. I watched as he came abreast of the street light. He turned and waved, I looked away and went inside.

# Chapter 15

Coffee in hand, I sat on the deck and watched the sun rise. A cloudless blue sky left me serene as I considered my conversation with Marcus. He'd caught me by surprise, and his well-meant advice had come from the heart. I was sure of it. We hadn't had that kind of communication in ages, and it left me feeling cared for. By the same token, I wasn't foolish enough to think we were on the best terms, especially since he remained a Rhode Island State Trooper, and I was still a wildcard at the best of times.

Indoors, I left my cup in the sink, a note for Lola, and left the house to walk into town. I went straight to Ballard's Inn and asked for Mr. Casella. The desk clerk leaned forward and pointed to the restaurant section of the hotel. "He just went in there. I believe that's him sitting by the window."

I thanked the clerk, walked through the restaurant doors, and approached Mr. Casella.

"Good morning, I'm Lavinia Esposito."

His brows rose a tad, he got out of his chair, and smiled as he shook my hand. "Please, join me, Ms. Esposito. Jack Casella, nice to meet you."

His dark, wavy hair, exceptional good looks, and knockout smile gave me pause. This man was so different from the last attorney Dad had sent, it caught me off guard. Aquiline features, a Roman nose, sculpted lips, and a body that showed he was sports-minded caught my attention.

He asked if I wanted coffee or breakfast and I told him I'd only have coffee. He ordered and then remarked, "Your father mentioned you were having a bit of trouble with law enforcement out here?"

"You could say that. I've been unfortunate enough to find three dead bodies, all from crime families, and the investigating officer would like to arrest me, even though I clearly had nothing to do with those deaths."

We sat back without uttering a sound when the waiter brought a fresh carafe of coffee and a cup for me. After he walked away, Jack leaned his elbows on the table. "You have been busy. I can see why Gino is concerned."

"How do you know my father?"

"We've had dealings in the past. My father and yours are long-time friends. When I finished law school, they both worked hard to get me established."

My curiosity was on the rise and I had a need to know more. "How was that?"

"It isn't really important, but if it hadn't been for our fathers, becoming an attorney in Rhode Island would have been an overwhelming and a more than likely impossible task. Similar to hair salon businesses, there seems to be an attorney's office on every street corner in the state. Differentiating oneself from such a huge number of lawyers can be daunting."

Still curious, and since his answer didn't really tell me anything definitive, I yearned to ask more. Unfortunately, I wouldn't have the chance.

Softly, Casella asked, "Were you aware of these men's connections?"

"Not immediately, only after they were identified and Officer Martin told me who they were. The last man, John Pacci, was a friend of my father's."

"Is Officer Martin aware of Gino's association with Mr. Pacci?"

I shook my head. "After I found Pacci, I called my father right away. That's when he said I needed a lawyer for my own protection."

"Did I mention I always thought Gino was a wise man?"

I laughed and drank my coffee.

"From now on, you're not to speak with law enforcement concerning the deaths of these people, or their connection to the mob. If anyone asks you a question concerning any of that business, tell them to contact me, understand? Gino has put your well-being in my hands, and I won't let either of you down." He handed me a business card and watched as I tucked it into my handbag.

"Have you ever worked with people involved in this type of situation?" I asked.

"My clients are varied and many. Don't worry, Lavinia, you're in good hands."

Again, he'd left my question unanswered, at least to my satisfaction, and the hairs on the back of my neck bristled. A call to Dad was in order. I thanked Jack for his advice, and before leaving, I said I'd heed it.

On my way through the marina, I came across Marcus and Aaron standing at the rail, their arms resting on it while they chatted amiably.

Sidling up next to them, I leaned my arms on the rail, too, and remarked, "What are you two up to?"

Both men looked in my direction and smiled.

"We were enjoying the view," Aaron answered.

I followed their line of vision. Two bikini-clad women sunned themselves aboard one of the boats tied to the dock. I bid them goodbye and started to leave.

In a flash, I was sandwiched between Marcus and Aaron as I strolled toward Nana's house. Jostled by them, I gave each an elbow in the ribs and asked what they were up to now.

"We thought you might need protection, so we'll walk you to Nana's, get a free bite to eat, and then visit with Little Miss Dynamite," Marcus said.

Where had this sudden good humor come from? I glanced at each man and smirked.

"What?" Aaron asked.

"You know what."

"Honest, we aren't up to anything other than what Marcus said."

"Yeah, right, as if I believe that. You two just *happened* to be hanging about, checking out the bikini girls when I *happened* along? Give me a break," I remarked.

"Who was the guy you had coffee with at Ballard's?" Marcus asked.

"My newfound friend, Jack."

"Jack who?"

"Just Jack," I said.

We'd topped the hill and started down toward Nana's house when Lola stood up from the beach chair on the dock and waved to us. We returned her wave in unison and picked up our pace to greet her.

? ? ?

Lunch was over. Beer and wine flowed like Niagara Falls, and I was feeling pretty silly, mostly from the amount of alcohol I had consumed. Marcus was giving Lola a hand clearing the table and Aaron sat staring at me, a look in his eyes that I couldn't fathom, or maybe I didn't want to.

The crunch of tires on crushed seashells brought us around to peer out the window. "Your best friend, Dave Martin, has arrived, Vin."

"Must be my good fortune at work again," I said in a snarky tone.

Martin knocked on the door, and I called for him to enter. When he did, he stared at all four of us and then asked if he could speak to me privately.

I glanced at the others and then nodded. Lola, Marcus and Aaron went out the side door toward the dock. I turned to Martin, motioned to a chair and murmured, "Have a seat."

"It would seem you and Lola are correct in your assumption that the men onboard the yachts are heavily armed. The Coast Guard paid them a visit on open water and their reception was anything but friendly. That said, all the guns were licensed and registered, so there was nothing to be done about the fact they were carrying."

I stood facing him from behind a vacant chair and played my fingers across the top of it as if it were a piano. "Why tell me this?"

"You've met with your attorney. I'm sure he's advised you to refrain from answering any further questions law enforcement might have concerning what's going on out here, but I would like you to know that I am not interested in arresting you for these murders. I also don't have an agenda where you're concerned. The island is generally a playground for summer folks, we don't have murder and mayhem here. We have drunken bar fights, boat-hopping parties, and the odd drunk driver. My department is a small one. The department isn't equipped for this type of thing, but the State Police and FBI are, so I've turned the entire investigation over to them. I just wanted to give you fair warning."

I sighed, glanced out the window at my three friends lazily stretched out in the sun, and then looked Martin in the eye.

Unwilling to whack him with the olive branch he was offering me, I said, "I'm not sure why you've come to tell me this, especially since we haven't had the best of relationships since I found Dembrotti's body. But I appreciate the fact that you took the time to do so."

"These men know you well, but make no mistake, if they have any inkling you're involved, you'll be fair game. That goes for the other side of the coin as well. The mafia isn't as kind as the police are. Am I right about all this?"

I dipped my head and said, "You are."

"Then it's a fine line you walk at the best of times."

"It would be if I was involved in any way with either party concerned, but I'm not. Thanks again for stopping by." The man had been dismissed, he knew it as did I. He gave me a nod and left.

This was a day of days. Marcus and Aaron had omitted the news that they were now solely in charge of the mob crap happening on the island, and Dave Martin had been decent enough to let me know as much. Why? I stared out the window as he drove away, and then went to join the others on the dock.

I drew abreast of them, plopped down on the dock, and stretched out. "Where's Nana?" I asked Lola.

"She took off not long after you did. She and her friends were heading to the mainland for some theatre event or other that includes lunch and dinner." Lola snorted and then grinned. "It's a senior citizen play-date kind of thing. I'm glad she takes advantage of those opportunities, especially since she lives alone and is getting up in years."

"Nonni does those trips as well, she tries to get my mother to go, but mom has enough to do with my shop and keeping up with the elderly residents' activities at the Senior Center."

"I guess Martin didn't get under your skin this time. Is there anything you'd care to share about his visit?" Marcus asked.

"He had nothing out of the ordinary to say." I sat up and crossed my legs Indian style while glancing from Marcus to Aaron.

Marcus, not one to immediately look away, held my stare for a few moments. Aaron gave me a long look, and then, shading his eyes, he looked off across the marsh. "Looks like the birds are having a get together." Aaron pointed to the gulls flocking in and around the edge of the marsh. Silently, I prayed they weren't feasting on another corpse, good grief.

All four of us stood on the dock, eyes shaded with our hands to watch the gulls bicker over who was getting what first when one of them spread its wings and flew off with a gigantic fish in its beak. The others followed as though there might be a chance the first gull would drop his catch.

I brushed my hand across my brow when I realized I'd been sweating over the fact there might be another dead guy lingering in the salt marsh. When I glanced at the others, it was apparent they'd had the same thought. I started to laugh, mostly from relief, but also from the way we'd all come to the same, though wrong, conclusion.

"For a minute there, I thought we had another body," Lola said.

Difficult as it was, I remained quiet and listened to Marcus and Aaron chime in.

"You must be relieved, Vinnie." Aaron remarked with a grin.

"I'll say," I said and snickered.

Keeping my eyes on the men, I asked, "What's up with you two for the rest of the day?"

With a shrug of his shoulders, Aaron said he didn't have anything special going on and then he looked at Marcus.

"I'm on duty later." He glanced at his wristwatch and then said he should be getting back to change for his shift.

"We'll be going to Old Harbor Point and then out to dinner. Maybe we'll see you then?" I asked.

Glances passed between the two lawmen before I snorted and said, "For law enforcement, you two can't seem to keep yourselves together for one minute. We're aware you two have taken over the investigation from the local cops and that you'd do anything to figure out what Lola and I know, so why not fess up and stop playing these games?"

By this time, my hand had snuck to my hip, I'd flipped my hair off my shoulders, and even though there was a breeze, I was hot under the collar. *Geesh, couldn't they own up to one single thing?* Did everything have to be cloak and dagger? Really? Lola stood by in silence watching the scene play out without becoming involved. Smart move, since she was unaware of what Dave Martin had told me.

"Vin, don't get upset. You know we can't talk about ongoing cases, or at least you should by now," Marcus remarked.

"When were you going to tell me Dave Martin had relinquished his responsibility in the mob goings-on? By the way, he doesn't trust either of you very much, and from where I stand, I can't blame him." I stepped close to Aaron and looked into his eyes. "If you plan to try and trap me or my family in what's going on out here, you just remember our conversation. You've left me to get out of some tough spots in the past due to your *job*, but I won't accept any excuses this time around, is that clear?"

Marcus and Aaron asked, "What spots?"

Narrow-eyed, I stared at Aaron. "How about the time I was being chased from Tony Jabroni's house by a killer, and narrowly escaped an attack by his neighbor's Doberman? Where were you? Why, looking out the window of the house across the street, of course. Did you come to my aid? Not likely. Why? Because of your *job,* that's why. So take this as fair warning, both of you, if I get even one hint that you are setting Lola or me up as bait for the mob, or that you plan to arrest my father for some stupid association you think he might have with the bad guys, you'll both be sorry."

While I was on a rant, I wasn't angry, I hadn't raised my voice, and had managed to remain calm instead. Neither man knew what to do with me when I acted this way. They preferred to deal with the hot-headed Italian side of me, instead. I gave Lola a sneaky peak from beneath my lowered eye-lashes and saw her smile before she turned away.

Marcus laid a hand on my shoulder. "Okay, whatever you think is going on, is not going on. We plan to protect you and the other people on the island. It isn't an easy job with the limited number of people we have to help us, but we'll do the best we can. Aaron has reinforcements arriving this evening, they'll land very soon. I have no one except my partner, so we can do very little to assist. I, for one, have no intention of dragging you into a mobster situation, believe me, Vin."

His hazel-greenish brown eyes were earnest and I nodded, as did Lola. "I'm merely warning both of you. No tricks."

They nodded and I turned away, walked toward the house and heard Marcus say goodbye to Lola. Crushed sea shells crunched as he walked from the yard, I stood at the front door and when he looked back, I gave him a small wave. He offered a nod and went on his way.

After Aaron left, Lola and I rummaged in the fridge for a snack, poured wine and then we sat outside in the waning sun. Having emptied my wine glass, I set it on the arm of the Adirondack chair and listened to Lola go on about having dinner.

When I hadn't spoken, she stopped talking and stared at me. "You really gave them some crap earlier. What was that all about, anyway?"

I explained Dave Martin's visit and what he had said about Marcus and Aaron. How they might think she and I were involved with the mob, and that we'd be fair game by both sides, should we become suspect by either law enforcement or the gangsters.

I heaved a sigh and said, "For heaven's sake, I can't get away from those people, no matter what. I bet if I was stranded on an island in the middle of freakin' nowhere, there'd be a mobster hiding in a palm tree."

Lola started to giggle, her laughter sounding like sweet chiming bells, and I laughed at my own absurdity.

# Chapter 16

Dusk had descended as we drove to the Atlantic Inn Restaurant for dinner. We'd decided to sit on the veranda and take in the stunning view of Old Harbor and the ocean beyond the lawns. Patrons and guests filled every nook and cranny of the hotel, and I was glad we'd made a reservation.

The waiter handed us menus, took our wine order, and then left us to figure out what would best suit our appetites. Ultimately, I ordered striped bass and Lola chose the North Atlantic cod. Happy with our selections, we sat back and viewed the scenery when I heard a familiar voice behind me. "May I join you?" Jack asked.

Both, Lola and I turned at once to stare at Jack Casella.

We nodded and the waiter pulled out a chair for him. Once seated, he ordered a drink, perused the menu, and then ordered steak for dinner. Lola couldn't take her eyes off the man, and he had a difficult time pulling his gaze from her. It's the Julia smile that gets them. All men become stupid when she smiles. I admit, I was envious.

I made introductions, listened to them converse as though I wasn't in the room, at the same table, or on the same planet. Momentarily, I felt I was having an out-of-body experience where I hovered overhead and listened to what they said. Angels do that, right? Guess I would miss that boat, or maybe it had already sailed.

At some point, I cleared my throat and brought their attention to the fact that I was still sitting with them. Lola, with an unabashed grin, asked, "Is something wrong, Vinnie?"

I shook my head, gave her a smile.

Lola said she needed to visit the ladies room and excused herself.

While she was gone, I asked Jack where he'd studied law.

"Harvard, actually."

My brows rose and I gaped at the man. If he was of the working family sort my parents were acquainted with, how had they managed to send Jack to Harvard Law School? Even Brown University is above the means of many working class folks and difficult to get into, as is Harvard, no matter a student's grades.

"My uncle bequeathed me enough money to attend the school of my choice. My parents wanted me to attend Oxford in England, but I preferred Harvard. Where did you attend college?" His eyes held a sparkle of mischief and I realized he knew all about me.

"Roger Williams University is my alma mater. It's not as prestigious as Harvard, but I got one heck of an education there."

"So I hear. You have quite a reputation in the law enforcement arena."

"I'm sure," I said and laughed.

Lola returned. We leisurely enjoyed dinner, ordered coffee afterward and chatted about the mundane things in life that I never get to enjoy. If I had, I'm sure I'd have quickly become bored, and knew mundane was never going to be part of my lifestyle. The evening drew to a close as we rose from the table and said our goodbyes. To my surprise, Lola invited Jack over for breakfast the next day and he accepted the invitation with alacrity. I hid my grin as I realized not only Lola was smitten, but so was Jack Casella. We parted ways in the parking area and Lola drove us to Nana's.

We arrived as Nana was dropped off by her friend. The three of us went inside, all talking at once about our adventures. We agreed to change into comfortable clothes and meet downstairs again to continue our conversation. I reached the first floor and heard Nana say, "You seem quite taken by this young man. When will I meet him?"

"Tomorrow morning, he's coming to breakfast."

I grinned, thankful for the fact that Lola was no longer morose, lost in her misery of being the daughter of a don, and that she'd regained her good humor. I joined the women in the cozy parlor and settled onto the sofa, stretching out like I owned the place. Lola was in her usual chair and Nana had taken hers, where her knitting basket sat handy and she faced the television. I smiled a bit at the hominess of it all, and then asked Lola what she thought of Jack.

"Oh, gosh, he's so charming, and very pleasant. You don't mind that I invite him over, do you?"

"Not at all, it will be a nice change. Imagine if Aaron and Marcus walk in and he's sitting there? The conversation might get very interesting."

Her sudden intake of breath meant Lola hadn't thought that far ahead. "Maybe I should call and cancel."

"Absolutely not. I couldn't care less if they come by while he's here. Do you, Nana?"

She looked at Lola and gave her a grin. "Vinnie's right, it would be interesting, but if they don't show up, it could be even more so."

With that, Nana talked about her day, the play and dinner, and said how glad she was to return to the island. "I doubt I'd be able to stand living on the mainland. Too busy for me. At least here, we only have tourists from June to September with a few stragglers after that, but when it gets cold, they all run back home. I look forward to that time of year, when there's nobody blocking the sidewalks or streets."

Afraid we'd outstayed our welcome, I said as much. Lola gave me a look that said she'd had the same thought.

"Nana, if we've stayed too long and disrupted your routine, we'll pack up and go. No problem."

"Pshaw, don't you worry about me, you girls are welcome for as long as you want to stay. I get a kick out of the way Vinnie handles the police, the dead bodies, and the mob."

"Wh-what?" I stammered.

"You don't think I'm unaware of what's been going on around the island, do you? Why just the other day, Marilyn Huckley told me you found a mobster on the beach below her house. I knew before you even got home. We live on a small island. It's like those tiny English villages you see on those PBS mysteries, where all the busybodies know what's going on before the police do."

She slapped her knee and seemed to be enjoying herself at our expense. So much for guarding Nana from bad news. I smiled, said I was glad she knew what had been taking place, and then excused myself for the evening. I had a phone call to make and wanted to get it over with.

The night was cool and quiet. Water lapped the posts holding up the pier while I dialed my father's number. His gruff voice came across the line.

"Are you okay, Lavinia?"

"For the moment. I have some questions for you, and I really need the answers, so please don't hang up or sidestep, okay?"

"Fine, we're overdue for this talk anyway."

Oh gosh, was my father going to tell me he was a mobster? My heart squeezed, it became difficult to breathe, and I nearly fainted. Gasping for air, I heard him say, "Your mother is out so we can speak frankly."

*Oh my.*

"What do you want to know, Lavinia?"

"Are you involved with the mob?"

"In what way?"

"You know what I'm asking," I said.

"No, I'm not. What else?"

"Who is Lola's father?"

"Lavinia, I . . ."

I interrupted him. "No excuses. Just tell me."

"Jimmy Byrne."

"The Irish mobster from South Boston?

"Yeah, how do you know about him?"

"His name came up in conversation," I said and remembered Dembrotti's ghost telling me about him.

"He's cruel. You stay away from him, I'm warning you."

"I will, I really will, Dad. How do you know him?"

"He and Johnny Boy were associates of a sort."

"Surely not alliances?"

"Sort of, but I can't say more than that."

"He's on the island, isn't he?" I needed to know.

"If he isn't yet, he will be. Why?"

I told him about the sinking boat, the open water search of a boat by the Coast Guard, and waited to hear his thoughts. It didn't take long.

"That creep is nuts, he's deadly on a good day and has no remorse, none at all. Can you come home or are the police continuing to limit you to the island?"

I crossed my fingers and toes and then said, "I can't leave yet."

"You better not be lying, Lavinia. The people who are coming to Block Island are the worst of the worst, and possibly the last of their kind. The FBI has seen to putting so many mobsters in jail, but some of them are so smart, they'll never be caught and if they are, they won't be convicted. They have too much dirt on agents, cops, and the like."

Anxious to know more, but unwilling to lie to Dad more than was necessary, I said, "Lola and I will be home as soon as we can leave. We're trying to keep to ourselves and aren't going to the parties on the water and stuff. One more thing, Dad, do Marcus and Aaron know about Jimmy Byrne?"

"If they don't, they probably have a good idea. I think Jimmy ordered Pacci's death."

I heaved a sigh, rubbed my forehead with my fingertips and wished I were anywhere but here at the moment. I really could use a set of angel wings, though I was certain that would never happen. I said goodbye and tucked the phone in my pocket.

I went indoors, slipped up the stairs on tiptoe, and found Lola sitting on my bed looking at yachts in the magazine I'd seen Johnny's boat in.

"Where were you? I thought you had gone to bed."

I tossed my jacket on a hook and said, "I called my father."

"How did that go?"

"Better than usual. He wanted to know when we'd be home. I put him off by saying we had to stay until we were cleared to leave. I hope Jack doesn't find out we can leave anytime we want."

"Your father would be pretty upset, wouldn't he?"

"Uh, yes, he would."

"So, what are you holding back? I can see you want to tell me some tidbit you learned from your father, so give it up, will you?"

I checked the hallway, closed the door tightly and whispered softly, "Fine, I asked who your father is."

Her eyes grew wide and darkened if that was even possible. "And?"

"He said Jimmy Byrne, an Irish don from Southie. Dad also said he's deadly, and that's on a good day."

Lola opened her mouth and I raised my hands. "Just repeating what he said."

"No, it's okay. I figure your father knows what he's talking about. So, it's Jimmy Byrne, huh? My mother lied about her relationship with Johnny Pacci to keep me safe." Lola flopped back against the pillows and contemplated the news. "Hmm, well that's that. Let's move on. I no longer want to find out more or be bothered by what's happened in the past."

"That's quite a turnabout. Are you sure?"

"Very sure. I have better things to do with my life than to worry about who my father is, or what he's about. My mother was right, I need to focus on the future." Lola snickered. "I'm really glad she went home, aren't you? One wild card at a time, and that would be you, is enough to deal with. Thanks for telling me."

I nodded and worried that Lola hadn't let the news sink in long enough to have made such a definite decision. If others realized who she was or sensed the connection between her and Byrne, then Lola's safety would come into play. The fact that he was a killer, as well as her father, left me wondering how she truly felt about it.

"Lola, are you sure you've made the right decision? You aren't the least bit curious?"

"Like I said, I need to focus on the future, not worry about a past I can't change.

I nodded in silence and worried a bit about her reluctance to face what might become a dangerous situation for her because of Byrne. While mobsters don't generally aim for civilian family members, but aren't above taking advantage of relationships either. As much as I wanted to believe Lola, I had a feeling we would have to face Byrne at some time or other, whether we wanted to or not. The island was small, and we couldn't hide at Nana's house forever, and we'd have to go out at some point or other.

Bidding me goodnight, Lola went off to bed, and I lay down in the spot she'd vacated, with a pen and notepad in hand to write down the things I knew—and what I didn't know. One list was longer than the other, and by the third page of notes, my inquisitive nature took hold.

Restless and unable to sleep, I lounged on the bed for a while and then got up and went downstairs. Donning a lightweight jacket, I settled on the pier and hugged my knees to my chest while contemplating the starry sky.

I'd started to relax when I heard footsteps on the pier behind me. Figuring it was Lola, I didn't turn to look and was very sorry I hadn't. A heavy hand landed on my shoulder and swung me to face its owner. I looked up and gasped.

A heavyset, dark-haired man stood over me, his face menacing in the moonlight. Instantly, I was on my feet, facing him squarely, nearly nose-to-nose. He looked like a thug, a well-dressed, armed to the teeth, kind of thug. All at once, I wished I was home. But unlike Dorothy, I didn't have on red slippers you click together and be magically transported. Besides, I didn't live in Kansas anyway.

He closed the gap between us, tipped his head in my direction, and murmured, "My boss would like to see you, Ms. Esposito."

Holding back from jumping out of my skin in fear, I slowly nodded my head and asked, "Who would your boss be?"

His obsidian eyes never flickered, like shark eyes they were cold and flat. Creepy, very creepy. I held my breath as I waited for him to answer me. He shifted his weight and looked me up and down.

"That will be for you to find out. I have my orders, so accompany me without issue."

Unwilling to create a scene, awaken everyone, and potentially put them in danger, I gave him another nod. Aware that I was walking into the devil's floating palace, I went with the man. My curiosity had taken flight, my nerves jangled like symbols that crashed together in a terrible way, and my heartbeat was out of control. If I wasn't careful, I might just soil my underwear. I shook my head. Perish that thought.

We walked along the road to his car that purred so soundlessly I hadn't heard it. I took the passenger seat and waited for him to walk around to the driver's side and get in. All the while I silently chanted that I could get through this. Fortunately, my inner voice was mute, so I didn't have to deal with it. We drove into town, parked near the walk where boats were secured and parties were in full swing.

We walked in silence, I stumbled, and the thug's hand gripped my arm vice-like. I regained my balance, gave him a look, like the one your mother gives you when you shouldn't be doing something, and he dropped his hand. He motioned me forward. I realized the party boats were far behind us, and we now approached a softly lit area where gorgeous, super expensive yachts were moored. No wild parties here, just the soft lapping of water against the sides of each craft.

Silently berating myself for not having had more sense than to stay in my bedroom, away from the possibility of becoming enmeshed in this type of situation, I went where directed, praying with each step I took.

I looked at the thug, then stared off toward the moonlit end of the pier. I could have sworn Dembrotti's ghost hovered just above the yacht. He didn't make any movement, just hung there, suspended in the night sky like the moon. I shook my head and drew a deep breath as I was escorted aboard the magnificent watercraft.

Once inside the double doors of the salon, the thug guided me toward a leather sofa that proved to be soft and supple under my body. I watched as he walked away.

He turned and said, "My boss will be in shortly, stay there." His dark-eyed gaze took me in once more, and then he left.

As dangerous as this could become, I found myself fascinated by my surroundings. The room was beautifully and sophisticatedly decorated. I soon realized Lanky Larry had worked on this boat as well as on Johnny Pacci's. That man certainly got around. Maybe after this was all over, I'd give the round butterball a call and ask how he'd become the sole artist for the mob? Beautiful pictures adorned the walls, and expensive, tasteful furniture was set in strategic places.

I stood up to peer out the windows and heard a soft tread across the floor. I turned, gaped at the man walking toward me, and knew I'd met Lola's father, Jimmy Byrne.

Daughter and father resembled one another so much, there couldn't be any mistaking them as anything other than relatives. His hair was a more burnished copper color than Lola's, but the sprinkle of freckles, the smile, the darker than dark eyes were unmistakable.

He reached a hand out to me and said, "So you're Lavinia Esposito? I'm glad to make your acquaintance."

On dangerous ground, I knew better than to be flip, so I shook his hand, smiled and acknowledged him for who he was. "You are Jimmy Byrne, correct?"

He gave a slight nod.

"You look like your aunt. She was truly a wonderful woman, you must miss her."

I agreed that I did, and said, "The resemblance between you and Lola is amazing. You two couldn't look more alike if you wanted to."

He motioned to the chair I had vacated and took one opposite me. He seemed relaxed, but all mobsters are fairly good actors, especially dons. They had poker faces that even the best poker players in the world couldn't fathom. No tells, no signs to indicate what they were thinking and even worse, no indication of what might happen next. Okay, that gave me pause.

"How is Lola? I hear great things about her. You aren't corrupting her with your inability to mind your own affairs, are you?"

I gave him what I hoped was a sweet smile and promised I wasn't corrupting her because she was incorruptible. I mentioned how charming and honest she was and that she ran a great deli in Scituate.

He listened, never took his eyes off me for a second, and then smiled the Lola smile. Good grief, no wonder people didn't know what was coming next. He charmed them into thinking he was the good guy.

"Her mother is a good woman, smart to get away from the likes of me, but she was wrong to keep Lola from me all these years, even though I do understand why. I would have put her through any college or university she wanted to attend, set her up in a magnificent business, and been her benefactor."

*Yikes.* He'd have corrupted her for sure. Probably would have used her business to launder money, smuggle in stuff that had no place in her life. It was all on the tip of my tongue to say as much, but I refrained.

"In as much as that's true, Lola has done very well for herself. She's a lovely person, honest and true to her friends, and very charming. Truth be told, she has the same charming smile that you have." I let my gaze take in my surroundings, and then asked, "So tell me, why am I here?"

"Why, I want to meet her, of course, and you're going to make that happen for me, Lavinia."

*Boom!* Just like that a shock went through me and my inner voice chose that very moment to kick in. *Did you think this was a social call? Did you think he wanted to be your BFF? Get a grip.*

I sucked in a huge breath, and let it out slowly. While I thought the voice had a good point, I should have been smart enough to know what Byrne wanted. After all, who am I? Nobody, that's who. Simply a friend of his daughter. A daughter he's never formally met or been able to ruin. Why would he put her in danger? Couldn't he see how unfair that would be to her?

"I can see you have reservations concerning our meeting, Lavinia. Please feel free to say what's on your mind."

I waited a mere second or so, and then with as calm a demeanor as I could muster, I said, "She knows who you are, and has said she has no interest in knowing more. Don't you think you'd be placing her in peril by meeting with her? I understand why you want to get to know her, however, it might not be good for Lola to meet with you. She's had great difficulty coming to terms with the fact that Gloria's husband isn't her real father."

Maybe I'd said too much, or maybe not enough, but it was too late now. The words hung in the air like dense fog.

"Please, Lavinia, I don't plan to parade her around in front of my enemies. You'll bring her to the North Lighthouse tomorrow, where I will be waiting for her. You will do that, won't you?"

"If I say no, then what?"

"I'll figure out another way to see her, but you certainly aren't entertaining the idea of refusing me this one favor, are you?"

His look was cold and a bit curious, and if I played poker, I'd know that was his tell.

I leaned forward in the chair, elbows balanced on my knees, and stared at the mosaic design of the coffee table between us. His words had been uttered in the friendliest threatening way, his eyes were hard and shark-like, and he'd likely feed me to them if I wouldn't help him. Okay, I was in trouble, serious trouble, the worst I'd ever been in before. All my past problems with the mob paled in light of this. What else could I do, except grant his request?

"Let me say this, I will bring her, but she'll know who she's meeting. She's my best friend, and I don't want to see her hurt in any way. If she is, well, it won't be pretty for whomever hurts her."

He smiled again and dipped his head in agreement. "You are a true friend, Lavinia." He rose from the chair, looked back at me over his shoulder as he walked toward the outer deck and said, "One o'clock, be prompt."

I had been dismissed, I felt cowardly like a traitor. *Geesh.*

The same thug brought me back to Nana's and left me at the edge of the driveway. I didn't utter a sound and neither did he. I walked lightly over the crushed shell driveway and entered the house.

# Chapter 17

Softly closing the door, I started up the steps when a light clicked on in the kitchen and Lola remarked, "Been on an adventure without me?"

Panic zoomed through me, followed by fear. This fear thing was becoming a pain, a real pain.

I stepped back, went into the kitchen, and slid into a chair at the table.

"I couldn't sleep, so I went out on the pier to watch the stars and moon."

Her brows hiked. "And?"

"A man came onto the pier and ordered me to go with him into town."

"And?"

"Okay, okay, he was a thug, one of Jimmy Byrne's men. Scary guy, too. I had no choice but to go with him. Byrne and I had a very brief visit, and he insists that I bring you to the North Lighthouse tomorrow at one o'clock. I argued with him, respectfully, of course, but to no avail. He's nuts, Lola, he's really a sociopath. My father was right when he said he was deadly on a good day. I didn't dare refuse him, though I did say nobody had better hurt you or it wouldn't be pretty for them. He seemed to respect that, hard to tell."

"I'm not meeting that man, not now, not ever."

"Just give it some thought, okay? He didn't give me much choice in the matter, so I had to agree or find myself sleeping with the fishes."

Her thoughtful brown-eyed stare was followed with words that made sense, yet didn't thrill me. "I think we should call Aaron. This is more than we can handle, especially since dear-old-dad is a nutter."

The new Lola had emerged, the old Lola who was nervous over thugs and whatnot, was gone. Had my friend developed an alternative personality? Nah, she'd just grown a stronger backbone. Maybe it had been there before, but she'd never had to step up and use her strength as she did now.

"If you feel that strongly about it, okay, but I don't know what Aaron can do to help us out."

"I'll call him now, maybe he can come over," Lola said as she dialed the phone.

I watched her closely and saw the resolve in her eyes as she spoke with Aaron, asking him to pop in for a visit.

"It's important or I wouldn't ask," she said softly. Silent for a few seconds, she then said, "We'll have the coffee on, and please come in quietly. Nana's sleeping. It is two in the morning and she needs her rest."

I set the coffee pot to perk while we waited and pulled mugs from the cupboard. A tray sat handy so I put the coffee pot, warming pad, mugs, and milk on it, and took it into the cozy parlor.

Lola stood at the door, waiting for Aaron to arrive and let him in before he could knock. "Who has your truck?"

"I had one of the guys drop me off. That way Nana wouldn't hear the noise it makes when it rolls over the seashells. She isn't awake, is she?"

"No, and we're trying not to wake her, either," Lola whispered and led the way into the parlor with me tagging along behind. She shut the door and settled in after we'd all filled our mugs. I briefly explained what had happened, who Lola's father was, and what he expected from us.

When I mentioned Jimmy was Lola's father, Aaron's eyes widened and he openly gawked at Lola.

"I would never have guessed, unless I saw you two together. Now that I think about it, you do look a lot alike, Lola, though, that's where the resemblance ends. What would you like me to do about this situation? I can't very well arrest him for being your father." Aaron sat back on the sofa and drank his coffee.

I gave Lola a quick look and nodded. It was my way of saying I told you so. She rolled her eyes and said, "If I don't meet with him, he'll likely take it out on Vinnie and that will never do."

"I can have him watched when he meets with you. A couple of agents will be assigned to the beach in case things go awry. Otherwise, my hands are tied. It's not against the law to meet someone, unless of course, it's forcibly done." Aaron turned his eyes to me and asked if I'd been threatened.

"It wasn't what he said, it was what he didn't say and the look in his eyes." I shivered at the memory and slugged down more coffee, as if that would help.

"All right, two or three agents will be assigned to the beach early on so he won't be suspicious. They'll be picnicking, and you'll know who they are. One o'clock, right? Be there on time, and don't gawk at the people on the beach. Be calm," he said and stared at me.

"We will, but if he tries anything, I refuse to be held responsible for my actions. I just want you to understand that," I said.

Aaron nodded, smirked a bit, and then focused on Lola. "You're not happy about this, I can tell, but better to do this in the open rather than have him drag you to the yacht like Vinnie was earlier. By doing this, you're in public, can leave if you want, and you'll have protection if necessary."

"You aren't expecting me to become involved with him, are you? I'm nobody's pawn," Lola remarked.

"Why would you think that?"

"There was a time when you wanted Vinnie and me to work undercover with you to find out what was going on. Remember that conversation?"

He nodded. "That was before Johnny Boy was murdered."

Lola sipped her coffee and then said, "Just so you know, we're unwilling to become involved with these people. Johnny Boy might have been easier to deal with than Jimmy, so keep that in mind, Aaron."

He set his mug on the tray, rose from the sofa, and said, "I will. Just follow the plan and you'll both be fine." He leaned down, kissed our cheeks and then left as quietly as he'd arrived.

We lounged in our chairs, each lost in thought, when the door opened and Nana walked in.

"Was that Aaron Grant?" Her eyes were wide as she took in the scene.

"Yeah, he wants us to give him a hand with a plan he has for tomorrow." Lola glanced at the wall clock and then said, "Uh, later today."

"You girls need to get to bed. It's going on three and you have a guest coming for breakfast, Lola. Now go on upstairs."

I put the mugs on the tray as Lola headed upstairs. Nana watched as I started to walk from the room. When I drew abreast of her, she reached out and laid a hand on my arm.

"You'll protect my granddaughter, won't you?"

"That I will, Nana. No worries."

Nana gave me a slight smile and nod and headed for bed. I cleaned the coffee pot, set it up for the morning, and washed the cups. Would the meeting go well or was this a ploy by Jimmy to get Lola to trust him and then use her in his nefarious activities? Money laundering came to mind again, followed by other equally dangerous and unlawful deeds.

I'd climbed into bed, opened my laptop and searched for articles on Byrne. He was a man with a horrific, yet unproven record of assault, murder, and just plain bad things. His charges had never brought him to a courtroom, mainly because he was shrewd enough to make witnesses and evidence disappear without a trace. Even in today's world, where citizens were watched by cameras everywhere, phones were hacked as often as computers by law enforcement, Jimmy Byrne remained clean as a whistle. How, I wondered.

I set the laptop aside and snuggled under the coverlet. I must have dozed off, because Lola's light tap on the door woke me with a start.

"I'll be right there," I mumbled.

She opened the door and peeked around the edge of it. "You're a wreck."

"Was it a long day and night yesterday, or what?"

"For you, yeah. I'll be in the kitchen preparing breakfast for us and our guest. Get a move on, okay? I need a hand." She closed the door and scooted downstairs.

I slipped out of bed and took a shower. It was going to be a trying day, I just knew it.

??? 

Breakfast was ready, Jack showed up on time, and all went smoothly. When he lingered, I left him and Lola alone, thinking a walk would do me good. I'd gone about a mile from the house when a vehicle pulled up and stopped next to me. I shaded my eyes from the glare and saw it was Dave Martin.

"Good morning, Ms. Esposito."

"Good morning."

"Fine day, today," he said.

I studied at him for a second or two and then asked, "What's going on?"

"Get in the truck, please."

"Why?"

"Because I asked you nicely."

My curiosity soared out into the universe. I went around to the passenger's side of the vehicle and climbed into the SUV. I buckled my seat belt and sat waiting for the axe to fall. The entire time, my mind zoomed over possibilities. Did he know about Jimmy Byrne and Lola's connection? Had Aaron taken him into his confidence? I dismissed that question immediately. Was he going to arrest me after all? For what? I opened my mouth to speak but he interrupted the questions that were sure to spew forth.

"Another body has been found."

"Holy crap, you must be kidding."

"Not in the slightest. A couple of artists get together weekly to do what they call *plein-air painting*, which means they are outdoors."

"I know what plein-air means. Where did they find the body?"

We'd reached the cemetery and weaved through the narrow road that wound snake-like along the grounds. Three artists, painting gear at their feet, huddled together while Marcus stood several feet away with the dead body. I took a deep breath and waited as Dave stopped the truck.

I turned to Dave and asked, "Who is it?"

He shrugged and said, "Maybe you can tell us. There aren't any signs that he'd been thrown overboard, and he's in pretty decent shape, for someone who's dead, anyway."

We left the truck to join Marcus, and I looked down at the body. It was Rudy Santilli, a guy my father played cards with. Good grief, what was he doing here? I looked away from his deader-than-dead features and tried my best to avoid the bloody, gaping slice in his throat. I hurried to distance myself from the crime scene and my breakfast made a hasty exit. Good golly, I hate the sight of blood and even worse, I hate the sight of death.

"Do you know him, Vin?" Marcus asked quietly as he handed me a bottle of water and a hanky.

I shook my head in answer, rinsed my mouth a couple of times, and doused the hanky with water to wipe my face while taking time to assimilate Rudy's death. When I was finished, I straightened up, turned to him and said, "Never met him before. Sorry." I walked back to Martin, avoided looking at the Rudy, and knew Marcus was glaring at me.

With a cool, hard, stare, Marcus kept his eyes on me, it was evident he couldn't tell for sure if I had fed him a lie. All I could do was stick to what I'd said and go from there. Why was Rudy dead? Who'd killed him, and what was he doing on the island? Had he come for a stay with his family? Did he have a family? All I knew of him was his association with my father.

Martin's face held a questioning look. "You're sure, Ms. Esposito? You definitely don't know this man?"

Again, I shook my head and asked, "When was he found?"

"Shortly time before I picked you up. Why?"

I shrugged. "Just wondering how long he's been here, I guess."

Marcus put his hand on my arm and said, "Come on, I'll take you back to Nana's."

Martin stepped forward, put his hand on my other arm and said to Marcus, "I'm not finished with Ms. Esposito yet."

Held between the two men, my temper rose. I shook them off and glanced at each lawman. "Excuse me, but I think we *are* done here. I said I don't know the man, so what more could you want to know?"

"Have you ever seen him on any of the boats you've been on lately?"

I quelled the panic that was about to take over while I wondered if Martin, or someone from his police department, had witnessed my trip to Jimmy's yacht the night before. "Not that I remember, sorry."

Martin pressed his lips together in a flat line. His expression seemed one of dismay. "You can go, but stay on the island."

"I will." I glanced at Marcus and said, "Let's get going, Lola must be wondering where I am."

We drove along the narrow road, and parked in Nana's yard. The front door flew open and Lola raced across the yard.

"Are you all right?"

I smiled at her concern. "I'm fine, really. I'll tell you about it later." I turned to Marcus. "Thanks for the ride. Sorry I couldn't be of more help."

"You better hope I don't find out you're lying to me, Lavinia. It's against the law to impede a police investigation." He tipped his head as if to tell me to get out of his vehicle, and without another word, I did so.

I slung my arm around Lola's shoulders and we marched toward the house. We heard Marcus leave and before we reached the front door, I steered Lola out onto the pier. We sat in the beach chairs, let the sun warm our faces, and I explained what had happened.

"You'll never believe who it was," I said.

"Well, tell me, don't keep me waiting."

"My father's friend, Rudy Santilli. You know, he played cards with him at the K of C Hall."

"That sweet man was murdered? No way, why would anyone do that to him? He couldn't have been a nicer person." Her expression sad, Lola seemed on the verge of tears.

Since we had worse things to deal with today, I said, "Buck up, because I do believe the worst is yet to come."

She hauled in a deep breath and nodded in agreement. "You're right." Lola glanced at her watch. "We're meeting Jimmy in an hour. Is there anything we need to do in preparation?"

"Not that I can think of. I suppose Jack left after I went walking, right? When are you seeing him again?" I asked with a grin and a sly glance.

Her giggle was answer enough, she was smitten, and they'd be getting together very soon.

"We've got a dinner date tonight. You don't mind, do you?"

"Not at all, have a great time. I have to check in with the college anyway, since I agreed to teach a six-week class starting in August. Your date will give me time to work up the curriculum, and hopefully, I'll get a student roster when I call. Classes will be held at the Providence campus so I won't have to drive across the state to teach."

"I feel better about leaving you here, then."

We both turned our heads in unison as Aaron's SUV stopped in the yard. He got out and waved to us before sauntering across the grounds and onto the pier, a serious look on his face.

"Rudy Santilli was found murdered this morning. Marcus said you didn't recognize him. Vinnie, your father plays cards with the man, so would you like to explain why you lied?"

Caught out by a man who could tell when I lied, and he hadn't even been there for mercy's sake. So how did he know Rudy was friends with my father?

"Dave Martin and Marcus had no idea who the dead man was. How did you find out?"

"They ran his prints, I recognized him as a person of interest, and knew he was friends with your father. Why did you lie?"

Okay, so Aaron was annoyed, so what? I stood, stepped into his space and looked him in the eyes. "Because this very issue we're having now is what I was trying to avoid."

I stepped back and to the side, tried to get past him, but was caught by the arm in a vice-like grip.

"Not good enough, try again," he urged.

"That's all I have to say, so get over yourself, and take your hand off me."

He did as I instructed, gave me a narrow-eyed glare, and I walked away. My innards were quaking, my nerves tattered to shreds, and fear of what would take place in less than an hour left me shaking in my shoes. I climbed the stairs to my room, unhooked the charger from my cell phone and dialed my father's number.

Whether or not he was standing by the phone in anticipation of my call, Dad answered on the first ring.

"Lavinia."

"Dad, Rudy Santilli has been found dead in Block Island's cemetery," I said.

His silence was long and drawn out. Tapping my upper lip with my index finger, I waited, knowing he was absorbing what I'd told him. I could only imagine what ran through his mind.

"Come home, now, right now," he barked.

"I can't, the island police told me not to leave. They aren't aware I know him, except for Aaron, anyway. If he's told Marcus, well, he hasn't said, but I know he didn't tell the island police what the connection is between me, you, and Rudy. I know you and Rudy have been friends for years. I'm real sorry about his death. I'm quite worried about what's been happening out here. Is everything all right at home?"

"He was a good friend, a good man. Stay close to the house, don't ever be alone, and if that means you have to have Marcus or Aaron with you, then by all means do so. The minute you can leave the island, come home, understand?"

"I do, I understand. It was awful to see Rudy dead."

"How was he killed?"

"Someone slit his throat. It made me sick to my stomach. Lola's very upset, as well."

"Do you have any other information?"

"No, just what I've told you. Was he here on vacation with his family?"

"He doesn't have a family. His relatives are deceased. I have no idea what he was doing out there, and, he never mentioned he was going to Block Island when we played cards last week. You be careful, Lavinia."

"Believe me, I will. I'll call you if I hear anything else, okay?"

He grunted, and the line went dead. I held the phone away from my ear and gawked at it, as I always seemed to. It's so rude to hang up without saying goodbye, but that was Dad's way of ending a call.

A light tap on the door sounded before Lola peeked around the edge of it. "Are you ready to go? It's nearly one, and we must be prompt, remember?"

I nodded, grabbed a pair of sunglasses, and tucked the phone into my pocket on the way down the stairs.

"Where's Nana?" I asked.

"She's gone to her book club meeting. For a small island, the ladies sure do stay busy, especially the retired ones, like Nana."

"It's good that she gets out so often, especially at her age. She must be in her eighties, huh?"

Lola nodded as we coasted to a stop on Corn Neck Road and parked the car. We started along the walk and noticed a slew of sun-bathers and swimmers enjoying themselves. Two couples sat together, shared a picnic, and I wondered if they were the agents Aaron had said would be present. I didn't turn my head in their direction, but slid my eyes back and forth behind the sunglasses to see who was where and how many people there were.

Another car had pulled to a stop and car doors closed with a *thunk* as we reached the North Lighthouse. I stopped to read the plaque while Lola glanced around in search of Jimmy.

"Did you know this lighthouse was erected in 1867?"

Lola turned and asked, "Should I care about that right now?"

"I was merely trying to ease your mind with some trivia. No need to get snappy."

"Sorry, Vin, I'm a train wreck. I just want to get this over and done with."

We turned away from the plaque and noticed we had company. How had they crept up without us hearing them?

Not far from us, two goons stood with their legs spread, hands clasped in front of them, seemingly at ease. They wore sunglasses, so it was hard to tell what they were thinking, if it was at all possible.

"Ms. Trapezi, would you and Ms. Esposito accompany us?"

"To where?" I asked.

"This way." The first goon ushered us around the side of the lighthouse onto the sand. A yacht floated off Sandy Point, and a motorized dinghy had been hauled ashore. Lola peeked at me as she lowered her sunglasses to look at me. I shrugged, and moved forward. There was no chance of turning back now, I was sure we'd be forced to go with these men should we refuse.

Even from this distance, I could see someone standing on deck, binoculars held up to his face, and guessed it was Jimmy Byrne.

# Chapter 18

Though my nerves were shot, and Lola was a wreck, our ride to the yacht was brief. The sun shone gloriously as we rode the waves. Wind whipped through Lola's locks, and while I'd tried to secure my hair, the mass of curls was wild and tossed by the time we slowed and left the dinghy behind.

We both finger-combed our hair, to no avail, while we waited to be led into the salon where I was sure Jimmy would receive us. It was his opportunity to act like a king. We walked through the double glass doors and I struggled to hold back my laughter. He sat majestic-like in a chair, and I wouldn't have been surprised if he'd been wearing a crown. Arrogant twit that he was.

He dipped his head a tad and our two escorts left the room. Never taking his eyes off Lola, Jimmy beckoned us forward. We stood in front of him like servants, which aggravated the daylights out of me.

"Please, take a seat," Jimmy said as he waved his hand toward the two chairs near his.

I took one chair, Lola sat in the other, and we waited in silence for his majesty to speak. Lola arched her brow a bit and I smirked.

"I asked you here today in order to meet you, Lola, on my own terms. It is unwise for others to know we are connected in any way, you're aware of that, aren't you?"

"I am. Frankly, if it had been up to me, I'd have avoided meeting you at all costs," Lola remarked.

My nerves tightened. This auburn-haired firebrand was about to take on the deadliest mobster of all, at least in my opinion. Here we were, out on open water where sharks swam around in search of tasty morsels, and Lola had decided to wave a red flag in front of this Irish bull. What was she thinking?

His soft laughter made my nerves even more taut.

"You're more like me than you think. I like your outspokenness."

"Other than an uncanny resemblance, I doubt I'm anything like you. What do you think, Vinnie?"

Oh boy. She would have to ask me this. Internally, I squirmed, externally, I smiled and said, "Your resemblance to Jimmy is uncanny."

Her eyes snapped with anger. Oh yeah, this was not going to be a warm, friendly visit. Our day was headed down the toilet, fast, very fast.

"Now that we've agreed you are my daughter, I would like to say that I will have no further contact with you, for your safety and my own. You see, I realize you both have ties to the law, and it wouldn't bode well for any of us to be put in an uncomfortable situation where you or Lavinia would be forced to spy on me and my enterprises."

Her eyes wide, Lola blustered, "What makes you think I care enough about you, your businesses, or law enforcement, to gather information for them? I have no interest in any of that."

His gaze cooled at her question, though he remained calm. "Very well, then I can count on you to keep your distance?"

"Absolutely. Don't ask for favors, don't drag me into your *enterprises*, and don't bother me, understand? I enjoy my life, and it doesn't include you or your baggage."

Worried, I fidgeted in the chair and whispered, "Careful, Lola."

She gave the slightest of nods and stood. "If that's all you have to say, then we'd like to return to land."

Silent, Jimmy studied her for quite some time, his best poker face in place, and I couldn't read his thoughts. The man was good at what he did, otherwise, he'd have been behind bars by now—or swimming with the fishes. Ruthless, cunning, charming, deceitful, and other descriptive terms skidded through my thoughts as I regarded the man who could have us killed and tossed us overboard with the snap of his fingers.

My stomach tightened, I reached for Lola, gave her arm a gentle squeeze to say *shut up*, and said, "Thank you for inviting us aboard today, Jimmy. You're correct in your assumption of how unwise it would be for you and Lola to be seen together, or to have your connection known. We understand completely and appreciate your thoughtfulness. You can be certain neither of us will utter a word to anyone."

Okay, so I was nearly begging for peace between the three of us. Lola had set him straight about how she felt, and while that was well and good, it was also dangerous.

With a dip of his head, Jimmy rose and escorted us to the lower deck of the yacht and asked, "Would you care for a drink, or something to eat before you leave? I can have my man prepare something for you."

Lola stopped dead, and then said to Jimmy, "We've had lunch, but thanks for the offer."

I breathed a sigh of relief that Lola hadn't gone off on a tangent, had followed my lead of courtesy to a man who could make us disappear in a blink of any eye, and gave Jimmy a warm smile. At least, I hoped it was warm. It could have been a fearful smile, since that's how unstrung I'd become. This mob crap was out of control, as were Lola and I.

The tethered dinghy bobbed in the water against the yacht. I hurried to board, with Lola fast on my heels, and took a seat. Lola sat close and murmured, "Sorry Vinnie, I know I was reckless."

"We'll talk later," I said softly.

She nodded and we held on as we launched into the now rough waters on our way to the beach. Pushed willy-nilly by wave after wave, a huge swell caught us unaware, broke over the bow and half-soaked me to the skin. I shook my left arm, wiped my face with my dry right hand, and felt the left side of my hair that was plastered to my head. Lola laughed outright, as she was merely damp since I'd taken the brunt of the wave, and I laughed with her.

Most of the beach goers still sunned themselves, though a couple of people watched us approach the shoreline. I thanked the boat captain for our ride, waited for Lola to climb from the craft, and followed her lead. I pushed the boat into deeper water for the motor to catch without churning up sand and stalling. The man gave me a nod and turned back toward the yacht.

I waded through shallow water onto the beach and waved to the people who lazily lounged under a huge umbrella. One of them was Aaron Grant, I'd recognize him anywhere, sunglasses or not.

"Can we join you?" I asked before plopping down on the beach blanket.

"You're soaked," he said and flung a towel in my direction. "You do realize you've blown our cover, right?"

"Not necessarily. I'm sure Jimmy is well aware he was being watched. Why do you think he didn't come ashore?" I snickered and then turned to Lola, who had unceremoniously, plopped down next to Aaron.

"Are you in a better frame of mind, now?"

She grimaced, said she was getting there, and gave me a lopsided grin. Her humor was on the way to complete restoration now that our visit with Jimmy had been concluded.

"Anything you'd like to tell me, Lola?" Aaron asked softly.

"The whole meeting thing was a joke," she remarked with disgust.

"Why?"

"Byrne wanted to get a look at me, sum me up, and when he had, he then advised me to stay clear of him for my own health. He wouldn't rescue me if someone was to find out about us, and I wouldn't want him to. He's a creep, a low-life, and I won't be dragged into that world. I think his main concern was that I would dog his every step to get close to him. Spare me, that would be the last thing I'd ever consider." She sat up, then rose and added, "I'm going home. I have a date tonight and need to get ready. Are you coming, Vin?"

About to agree, Aaron interrupted with, "Vinnie and I have unfinished business from this morning to discuss. I'll bring her back. Have fun tonight, Lola, you could use some after your harrowing day."

She grinned and said she'd see me later. I watched Little Miss Dynamite cross the sand and drive away in her Cooper.

Aaron's counterparts were preparing to leave. They'd begun to pack up the picnic basket when he stopped them and said he'd take care of everything.

We were alone, the yacht had disappeared from view, and I quietly sat regarding the Atlantic. Waves rolled in, the sound of the surf mesmerized and relaxed me. Thankful for that, I thought my mental cheese had finally slid off my cracker, and that would never do.

I stretched out and leaned back on my elbows watching ocean. Aaron foraged in the cooler and then handed me a beer. It tasted good, was cool, crisp, and tingly on my tongue.

"Thanks, I needed that. Got anything to eat?"

He dug into the picnic basket and said, "Just cheese and crackers, I'm afraid. The agents ate while waiting for you and Lola to return. It seemed you were on board forever, though, it was only a half hour or so. Tell me what happened, or we can discuss the lie you told Marcus this morning."

I accepted the scant fare he offered and then gave him a rundown. I commented on Lola's attitude and outspokenness.

"Lola's really come a long way from being the naive woman I met when I first came to Scituate. She's still adorable, though."

"I'm not talking to you about Rudy Santilli, but I will say I think aliens have abducted the real Lola and replaced her with this one. Honestly, she took on Jimmy Byrne like nothing I've ever seen her do before. Rude, she was rude, kind of aggressive, even. So not Lola, if you get my meaning. She was quite frank with him, I thought we were going to be fish bait."

"I've never seen you as insecure or nervous as you are now, Vinnie. Lola can handle herself, she's never had to until lately, but she's always been capable of it. Don't worry, that woman would be fearsome if pushed. I'm surprised you never recognized that trait in her, especially since you two have been friends for so long."

"I know, right? She's been so brave and willing to stand up for herself these days that I don't have to interfere on her behalf. Though, at one point, I felt she'd gone too far with Jimmy and put my hand on her arm as a warning to stop talking, which, thankfully, she did."

"You must have been shocked by her treatment of Byrne. He didn't even flinch, huh?"

"Not once. As a matter of fact, he seemed to enjoy her spirit and said they were more alike than she thought. That was met with a huge amount of derision. As the conversation progressed, I became quite alarmed by her attitude and know from my own mobster experiences that it doesn't pay to be flippant."

The sun had moved past the bluff and the sand had begun to cool. The crowd thinned, leaving me and Aaron behind. We folded the blanket and secured the umbrella with its strap, picked up the cooler and picnic basket, and trudged toward Aaron's Yukon.

He packed everything into the back of the SUV and then slowly drove to Nana's. I enjoyed the peace and quiet of the ride, figuring he was deep in thought over what had taken place between Lola and Byrne. He drew to a stop in Nana's yard and walked me to the door.

"I'll pick you up around eight for dinner . . . if you'd like to go, that is."

I nodded, said that would be fine, then asked, "We've had some disagreements during my stay on the island, why would you be interested in taking me to dinner?"

"I think you need a break. While we have had some issues, you're stressed, and I think an uncomplicated, relaxing evening out would do you good."

His answer was a good one, and even if I didn't quite believe it, I could use some time out. I would work on class lesson plans until he arrived. "Fancy dress or casual?"

His grin was sweet. "Casual. It's an island, remember?"

"See you at eight, then." I turned and entered the house.

The sound of laughter came from the sunroom as I reached the kitchen. I followed it and found Nana and Lola chuckling. This was the first real look of great humor I'd seen on Lola's face today. Pleased she was back to her old self, I sprawled out on the sofa, and asked what was so funny.

"I was telling Nana about our ride in the dinghy. I thought we were going to be flung overboard when we hit that last wave and you got soaked."

With a chortle, I said, "Me, too. That water was ice cold and shocking when it hit me in the face. My clothes dried quickly though. Good thing I was on that side instead of you."

"Nana is going out with her lady friends tonight. Jack is picking me up at six, and you're on your own for supper, okay?"

"Sure, no problem." I got up, pulled my wild curls away from my face as I went to my bedroom. I hadn't mentioned dinner with Aaron. I wasn't sure why, but for some unknown reason, I'd kept it to myself.

When I called the college, they gave me the information I needed. I checked the website for a student head count, and noted the class was filling fast, which pleased me to no end. There was nothing worse than teaching a couple of students, rather than a room full. Student participation was paramount, and too few of them didn't work out very well. I'd only had that problem once in the very early stages of teaching criminal justice. Word of mouth had spread concerning the curriculum covered, and before I knew it there was a waiting list to get into my workshops.

Making notes on my laptop, I looked up when, ready for her date, Lola popped into my room to say goodbye. She looked happy and I said so.

Her freckled cheeks brightened to a sweet shade of pink as she admitted she was looking forward to this night out with Jack.

"You deserve an evening out with a handsome man who has eyes only for you, Lola. When you're in his presence, a million people could surround you, but he wouldn't see them. I think he's quite taken with you."

"Don't exaggerate, Vinnie. He's not that wrapped up in me."

I snorted and said, "Oh, yes, he is. You just don't see it. Go, have fun, and I'll see you back here later." Again I didn't mention Aaron and wondered why.

Lola grinned, skipped down the stairs and went outside as Jack parked the car. I watched their body language and realized Jack Casella might be the man Lola had been waiting for all her life. I hoped she wouldn't be hurt, or perhaps find out he wasn't what she thought he was, but there was only one way for her to find out.

I worked until seven, took a shower, did my make-up, struggled with my hair until it was no longer unruly, and then dressed in a lightweight pair of white, stretch-linen pants that stopped just above the ankle. I topped it with a long, white, fitted tank top, and put on a textured knit, open stitched, side button pullover of shrimp pink, that fell to my upper thighs. I finished the outfit with a pair of D'Orsay flats in light, metallic gray before adding a pair of pearl-drop earrings to complete the look of a relaxed, yet fashionable, outfit. I had hit a sale at the J.Jill store in the Providence Place Mall in late May that I'd brought with me. I hadn't thought to wear it until now.

Scribbling a note saying I'd gone out for dinner, and not to worry, I left it on the kitchen table for Nana and Lola just before Aaron drove into the yard. He came to the door, knocked, and then entered the house.

He took in my appearance with a long, drawn out look and grinned. "You're gorgeous."

"Thanks. Where are we going?"

"I thought Ballard's would be a good place. They have an excellent menu."

I nodded and wondered if we'd run into Lola and Jack. Hoping we wouldn't, I got into the Yukon and buckled up.

# Chapter 19

Dinner was a leisurely affair. Sangria flowed, and my meal was delicious. We both opted for lobster dinners and enjoyed every morsel. Satisfied with the food and company, I leaned back in my chair and regarded at Aaron.

He raised a brow and asked, "What?"

"Nothing."

"There's something on your mind. I can see the wheels turn."

"It has been pleasant to have dinner without talking about anything going on lately," I said softly.

"You're right, it has. You must be anxious to return to the mainland."

I fiddled with my fork. If he only knew how badly I wanted to get away from the island. As lovely as Block Island was, the mob had ruined my stay. To change the subject before the conversation turned to thugs, mobsters, and hit men, I said, "I spoke with the college today about my upcoming class in August. Quite a few students have already enrolled."

Going along with me, Aaron asked, "Will you be teaching in Portsmouth?"

"I'll be at the downtown Providence campus, and closer to home."

"I wondered if you've ever considered moving."

Dumbfounded, I stuttered, "Wh-what? Move to where?"

"Out of state."

"Don't be ridiculous. Why would I leave Rhode Island? I have a lovely historic home, with no mortgage, in a sweet village."

He hesitated for a few moments. "You could always move away from the mob, Vin."

"Fat chance of that ever happening. Just the other day I told Lola that if I found myself on a deserted island, there would probably be a mobster hiding in a palm tree. That's how my luck runs."

He tone serious, he asked, "What if I was transferred? Would you consider making the move with me?"

My pulse hiked as my nerves tightened. "Are you being transferred?"

He shook his head. "You didn't answer the question."

"No, sorry."

"Why not? Is it because things are better between you and Marcus?"

I squirmed in my chair as I stifled a sigh. He'd put me on the spot. Forcing myself to face him squarely, I softly said, "Marcus and I have a connection. He and I might not be marriage material, if that's what you want to know. More like gasoline and a match at times, than roses and sunshine, we manage to get along."

"Who fits the roses and sunshine theme?"

"Other than my parents, I have no clue."

He reached across the table and took my hand in his.

"It wouldn't be you and I, then?"

"We get along much better than Marcus and I do. You're not as judgmental, and that means a lot to me. You are who you are, and while I can deal with that, the facts remain simple and clear. I'm invested in my relationship with Marcus now that he's not under such pressure at work. Besides, you are after my father for something you and your FBI cronies think is true. I often wonder whether your attraction for me is driven by the need to arrest him."

I put my frankness down to all that had occurred on this island and what still might.

"You believe I would use you to get to your father?"

Twisting my napkin, I concentrated on the table. "I do."

He leaned away from me. "It's not true, but I realize I can't convince you of that."

"I'm afraid not."

Aaron heaved a sigh. "We are friends, though."

"We are."

I fumbled for my purse, pushed my chair back and said, "Excuse me, I'll be right back." I left the table in search of the ladies' room. I pushed through the door and bumped into Nana.

She stumbled backwards. I reached out and pulled her upright before she fell.

"Nana, I didn't know you were coming here for dinner. How wonderful!" The words sounded weak, even to me.

"Are you alone? You could join us if you'd like, we're sitting outside on the deck," Nana offered.

"No, thank you. Aaron is waiting for me in the dining room." I scooted past her and into a stall. I heard the entry door swish and hoped she'd left. Unfathomable guilt rolled over me for having kept my plans from Nana and Lola. I washed my hands and returned to the dining room. Nana was talking to Aaron. I approached the two of them and heard her sweet laughter.

"You're a charmer, Aaron, that's for certain. You and Vinnie have a nice evening."

He wished her well, and I took my seat.

"Would you care for a drink on the patio?"

"I think I've had too much to drink, but I would enjoy a ride to West Beach, if you don't mind. I'd like to walk the shore for a while."

"Okay, let's be off."

We rode in silence for a time, reached our destination, and left the SUV behind as we walked in the sand. The smell of salt filled the air, and the moon shined brightly. I wondered if this might be what heaven was like. All the while, I hoped we wouldn't stumble across another dead mobster.

Leisurely, we strolled the beach. I'd left my shoes in the truck and felt the softness of mushy sand under my feet. I curled my toes, then uncurled them as granules were caught between them. The breeze was calmer and warmer than it had been these past several days and gently brushed my face. I breathed deeply as we walked, then turned back to where we'd started.

This evening had been free of arguments, with no mobsters making demands. I guessed miracles could still happen. Bringing those thoughts to a halt, my internal voice started to nag me. *Don't be foolish, the night isn't over yet. You might be in for a surprise before it ends.*

*Yeah, yeah, shut up,* I whispered under my breath while hoping for one decent night, out of all of the bad ones I'd had lately.

"What's wrong?"

"Nothing, really."

"You're tense, I can feel it."

"I was thinking what it's been like since Lola and I arrived on the island, then I realized it wasn't over yet."

"Indeed. Let's be confident that no more bodies will show up, and the mob will complete their business, before they sail away."

"Wow, that's wishful thinking. Let's face it, there are some intense issues going on between the powers that be. I find it hard to believe we're done with it all. There are bound to be more as disagreements increase. We both know it. My concern is keeping Lola out of the line of fire, especially if anyone gets wind of who her father is. While the mob refrains from picking on their counterparts' families, they think nothing of using family members to achieve their own goals."

He stopped and faced me. "You're right. We'll keep a close eye on Lola to make certain she remains safe. She and that attorney have hit it off. She gets dreamy-eyed when anyone mentions his name."

"She does. I'd considered looking into his background but have decided against it. If I found out he isn't who we think he is, I'd have to tell her, and that would cause a breach in our friendship."

"A catch twenty-two for you, Vinnie. Lola deserves to know about him, good or bad, don't you think?"

"Not going there, Aaron. I'm simply not."

"If you're worried, then I could look into him."

The moon was bright enough to reveal his features. His forehead furrowed, his dark eyes glittered, and his mouth had tightened.

"Let me think about it for a day or so before you go ahead and dig into his life, because I know you will. Jack won't thank us, and neither will Lola."

"Sure."

"I mean it, Aaron. Just wait, okay?"

"If you say so."

"It's late, I think I should go back to Nana's."

He gave me a nod and we returned to the truck and drove to Nana's.

??? 

Lights blazed, both indoors and out, as we slowed to a stop in the yard. Martin's police truck was parked next to Lola's Cooper. Instantly, I was out of the truck, running toward the house with Aaron at my side.

I burst through the door and skidded to a stop on the hallway carpet runner. Lola sat at the table, shaking, crying, and inconsolable. Nana paced the kitchen, her body tense, and her eyes snapping with anger.

I reached out to Lola and took her hand in mine. "What's going on?"

"Jack was attacked as we left the restaurant tonight. He's been flown by a Medi-Vac helicopter to the mainland for treatment. I'm worried he won't make it, Vinnie." She burst into tears, sobbed, and fought for control of her emotions.

I knelt next to her chair and hugged her tightly. "Get yourself together. We'll figure out what and why of it all. Come on, you can do it, you're strong enough."

She nodded, hiccupped a couple of times, and drew back from me. Her puffy eyes, runny nose, and bright red face showed her distress. It angered and worried me to see her this way.

A shot of whiskey was set before her and she downed it in one gulp, then coughed and choked as the amber liquid as it burned its way into her gut. I patted Lola on the back and said a silent thank you to Nana for having given it to her.

Lola looked up at Nana. "Thanks, I needed that."

Martin, who stood in silence next to Aaron, stepped forward and pulled out a chair. I leaned against the counter while Nana and Aaron sat in the remaining two chairs. When Aaron asked if I wanted to sit down, I shook my head.

"Lola, we'll get to the bottom of this. The FBI and State Police are going to help me to find who did this to your friend, and why it was done. Did Mr. Casella have any enemies on the island?" Martin had his notepad in hand and pen at the ready.

"Not that I know of," Lola said. "He came here to help Vinnie, in case you charged her with a crime."

He nodded and scribbled. "Does he have mob ties?"

A shake of her head and a sniffle was Lola's answer. I looked at Aaron and nodded. He rose from the table, went out the door saying he'd return in a moment.

Martin watched Aaron leave and then he turned to me. I shrugged, and his attention centered on Lola once more. "You weren't friendly with Mr. Casella prior to his arrival on Block Island, then?"

Again, Lola shook her head and gave him a wide-eyed stare. "Surely you don't think he's involved with all that's been happening?"

"I don't know what to think. Was there an altercation between him and anyone that would lead to his being assaulted?"

"We had dinner and sat talking on the hotel veranda for a while before we walked to the parking lot. That's when two men came out of nowhere and grabbed him. They dragged him into a darker area of the lot and started to beat and kick him. I tried to stop them but was warned off."

Martin finished jotting his notes and then said, "Odd that you weren't attacked as well."

"I guess." When Lola rubbed her face with both hands, then sighed wearily, I stepped forward.

"What Lola needs right now is rest. She's traumatized over the incident, Martin. Could you come by tomorrow to finish questioning her?"

"Certainly." He tucked the notepad into his shirt pocket, along with his pen while focusing on me. He tipped his head toward the door. It was my cue to go outside to talk with him in private.

"Lola, why don't you go upstairs and change, I'll come see you shortly. Then you and Nana can wait for me in the parlor, okay?"

Their nods were my answer.

Outside, Martin swung toward me and said, "Forever the protector, aren't you, Vinnie?"

"What are you talking about?"

"Do you think I'm unaware who Lola's father is? For crying out loud, she couldn't look more like him if she tried."

I stepped into his space. "I have no idea what you're going on about, Martin. Start at the beginning, and by the way, tread carefully. This is my friend you're talking about."

He didn't move, blink an eye, or even seem to breathe. Martin simply glared. Yep, he was pissed off.

"I don't believe Lola for a minute. I think she knows who the attackers were and is protecting them."

"You're wrong. She's in love with Casella, she'd never allow anyone harm him if she could help it. You should come up with another theory."

"I wouldn't expect you to betray her, but then, Casella is your attorney, isn't he? Maybe you ordered this beating."

I inched closer until we were nearly nose-to-nose. Not so long ago, Martin and I had seemed to come to an understanding, what had happened between then and now?

"What's made you so hostile?" I asked softly.

His eyes narrowed. This couldn't be good, not for me, Lola, or anyone else I knew. "Ms. Esposito, you've brought nothing but trouble to my island since you arrived. I resent it, and would arrest you if I could come up with one shred of evidence against you. I know you and Lola are involved with the mob. You were seen with them on more than one occasion. Your fancy attorney isn't able to protect you any longer, so think about that."

He hadn't answered the question to my satisfaction, though I could understand his feelings over the island, and the havoc that those deaths had wreaked. They certainly wouldn't be good for tourism, which was Block Island's main income.

My hand had sneaked to my hip. "You think about it, because I don't need an attorney or anyone else to protect me, I manage quite well on my own. You will not harass Lola or Nana, understand? Neither of those women have anything to do with what's happening on *your* island. It's not smart to harass either of them."

"Are you threatening an officer of the law, Vin?" Aaron stepped up next to me, gently took my arm and pulled me to his side, away from Martin.

Without looking in Aaron's direction, I said, "Not at all, he's been tossing around threats of his own, along with unfounded accusations, and it's unhealthy.

"Maybe you should go inside and check on Nana and Lola, Vin. I'll be in shortly."

"Fine." With a nod at Martin, I said, "Remember this conversation." I turned and walked away.

# Chapter 20

The two women were sitting side-by-side on the sofa when I entered the room. Lola had regained her composure, as had Nana. Gone was the intensity Nana had shown when I'd arrived at the house with Aaron. I smiled and took a seat opposite from them.

With determination, I said, "Tell me."

"Vin, it happened just like I told Martin."

I leaned forward, elbows resting on my knees and murmured, "Not quite, though, right? You left out a thing or two, didn't you?"

Lola's silence went on for a bit while I waited for her to gather the gumption to tell me the truth. It had to be bad since she needed time to get her thoughts together. While I waited, it occurred to me what a lousy a liar she was, and how glad I was for it, in case she tried to fib to me.

"You know I can't lie very well, so I won't try."

"Okay, then tell me."

"We were approached by two men in the parking lot, just like I said, only it was me they wanted instead of Jack. He protected me and was beaten to a pulp because of it." Lola drew in a deep breath, held it a moment, and then exhaled slowly, and managed to keep herself together.

"What did these guys want with you? Did they say anything?"

"They grabbed me by the arms and told me to come along quietly. I think they know who I am. When they tried to drag me away, Jack went nuts, and attacked them. They let me go, fought with him, and when they had beaten him senseless they came for me again. Essentially, I was saved by a group of people exiting the restaurant. They helped me with Jack after the two men ran off, and stayed until the medical rescue team arrived. Martin was right behind the ambulance and he brought me home after Jack was taken to the hospital."

"Did you recognize either man?"

She shook her head and then said, "Aaron, come on in."

I looked his way and saw he hovered in the doorway. "You heard, then?"

He said he had and sat in the chair next to mine to face Lola and Nana. "It's time for you and Vinnie to go home, Lola. It's not safe for you on this island."

Lola looked at him and said, "I don't think I'm safe anywhere, any longer."

"You might be right about that. Now that we know Jimmy is your father, I have to wonder what other mobsters have made the same association."

"My thoughts, exactly. I think I should meet with Jimmy tomorrow, if I can get onto the yacht, that is."

"Why? He probably already knows what's happened tonight and has taken steps to prevent it happening again. News in those circles travels faster than the speed of light," Aaron remarked. "Get some rest, all of you. I'll stop by in the morning." He rose from his chair, gave me a look and I followed him outside while Nana and Lola went to bed.

As Aaron opened the driver's door, he said, "My team is running a check on Casella. I doubt we'll find anything, but it's better to be on the safe side. I heard everything Lola said. I didn't want to interrupt her, so I remained in the hallway until she finished talking. She's in real danger now that certain people are aware of her identity. Stay close to her, Vin."

"You can bet I will. See you tomorrow, then. Thanks for a pleasant evening." I turned and then turned back. "What did you say to Martin?"

"I told him to pay no heed to your threats, that you were only concerned for Lola. I also said you have no idea of what's going on." Aaron gave me a keen look and said, "I have no control over whether or not he believed me. Good night, Vinnie." Aaron got into his truck and I watched him drive away.

Slowly, I peered around, looking hard to see if anyone lurked in the shadows. There was no movement, noises, or indication I was being observed. I went inside and checked the first floor, tested the window and door locks, and then climbed the stairs. The lights were out in Lola and Nana's rooms. Loath to disturb them after such a frightful evening, I went into my own room, shut the door, and called my father.

The phone rang a few times until Dad answered in a muffled voice. "What is it, Lavinia?"

"Jack Casella was brutally assaulted tonight. He was flown by helicopter to the mainland and is undoubtedly at Rhode Island Hospital since they are the major trauma center that's fully equipped to handle his injuries."

"How did that happen?"

My voice just above a whisper, I explained the event leading up to it and then listened as my father went crazy. He ranted for a few minutes, I had to hold the phone away from my ear for fear I'd go deaf.

I took a breath when he paused and said, "Dad, stop yelling, you'll wake Mom."

"You come home right now. Both of you. Right now, dammit."

"We can't come home right this minute, but we would like to know how Jack is doing as soon as you can find out, okay?"

"I'll get in touch with his father, I'm sure he's been notified. I'll get back to you by eight o'clock or so."

I glanced at the clock. Five hours to go before his call, if we could wait that long. "Thanks, Dad."

"You get back here as soon as you can. You and Lola, understand?"

"Yes, I understand. Good night." I hung up before he could, and felt better for having gotten that call over with.

I lay in the dark, my mind spinning at a hundred miles an hour. I must have drifted off since I woke up to bright sunlight streaming through the open curtains of my windows. Another sunny day on

Block Island. As I wondered what would happen next, the day seemed to dim.

Lola called from the bottom of the stairs, "Are you coming down for breakfast, sleepyhead?"

"I am, give me a minute." I rushed through my morning routine and scampered downstairs to have my first cup of coffee. Blessed is he who invented coffee. I scooped the cup from Lola's hand.

"You are such a coffee fiend," she said with a grin.

"Got a good night's sleep, did you?"

"Surprisingly, I did, but you didn't. You look exhausted."

I gave a nod and asked, "Have you heard from anyone concerning Jack?"

"Not yet." I glanced at the clock as my phone jingled. Dad was on the line.

"Jack was in surgery for a couple hours. He's in the surgical care unit and off the critical list. The doctors will keep an eye on him for a few more days before he's moved to a regular floor. He isn't awake yet, though, he's been heavily sedated. That's all the news I have. When are you coming home?"

"We have to get permission first. Thanks for calling, I appreciate it."

"Jack's a good man, he'll pull through. You can count on that. Tell Grant that he'd better find out who did this." The line went dead. Dad had spoken, so let the investigation begin.

My curiosity was on a roll, and we all knew what that meant. At least, I did. Friendly or not, Dave Martin would be my first tackle of the day. I wasn't afraid to take him on, and would have to muster every bit of charm I could find to encourage him to talk to me. We'd parted on less than friendly terms last evening, and for that, I'd have to work hard to find a common ground with him. He'd been unusually hostile while questioning Lola, had only offered the *my island* excuse as to why he was angry, and I had the sneaking suspicion there was more to his reasoning than he'd admitted.

After breakfast, I set out for a walk to the labyrinth. It was a calming place, lending itself to contemplation, and inner peace. Not that I ever had inner peace, but I had found some while there. I'd reached the rickety stairs and started to climb them as a truck slowly rolled down the hill and came to a stop. I had neared the top step. I looked down at Dave Martin and heaved a sigh. So much for calm, peace, and serenity.

"Join me, won't you?" I asked with hope he'd refuse.

"Go ahead. I'll join you in a minute."

Surprised, I turned and headed for the winding path. Many have reported the labyrinth can heal body and soul, and I heartily wished for that to reach Jack Casella while he lay in his hospital bed. I had begun to walk the path when Martin showed up next to me. He was silent while we did the ritual, ending with a seat on the bench under the overhanging shrubbery and trees. A sweet smelling breeze brought the scent of wild flowers mixed with salt air and I breathed the mixture deeply.

"I wanted to apologize for my anger last night. I'm frustrated by what's been taking place on the island and was wrong to blame you for it."

I gawked at the man and wondered if aliens had switched out Dave Martin. This alien thing was stupid, and I knew it, but I found swift changes in people's personalities a tad confusing.

"Wow, that's quite a turnabout, but I'm not complaining. I thought we had reached a place where we could be calm and open to one another. I also apologize for my reaction." There, I'd walked through the door he had opened, gave in, and now we'd see where my apology would take me. I leaned against the back of the bench and listened to the wind sigh, birds singing, and wished my stay on Block Island had been filled with only this type of thing.

"We haven't identified Casella's attackers. Casella is off the critical list, though he's being watched carefully at the hospital. I thought you might want to convey that to Lola."

"Thanks, I will. She's quite worried, and may have called the hospital by now. Who do you think did this to Jack, and why?" No way I would tell him it was Lola the men were after.

Martin shrugged. "No idea which mob family is to blame. Some of them are on their yachts, and others are at a couple of local hotels."

The local hotels tidbit was news to me. I wondered why Aaron had held his tongue where that was concerned. He probably thought I might visit the dons, but I'd had enough mob adventures to last me a while, and popping in for a quick visit wasn't on my To-Do list.

With a glance, I asked, "Where will your investigation go from here?"

"I'm not sure. Grant and Richmond are coming by this afternoon for a chat. I'll know more then. You and Lola are free to return to the mainland."

"Thanks. I'll let Lola know. She'll want to get back to see Jack as soon as possible. Just so you're aware, the times we were seen with the mob weren't something Lola or I initiated. We were approached and had no choice but to do as we were told."

His face was hard to read. "Were you forced?"

"Not exactly. We were asked, but the asking was done in a way that made refusal impossible. No weapons were displayed or threats spoken, but were intimated instead."

"Is your life like this all the time?"

I snickered. "More often than I'd like, that's for sure. I don't go looking for trouble. It just seems to find me."

"Grant said you suffer from a boundless amount of curiosity, is he right?"

Nodding, I chuckled.

"How does your family deal with your activities?"

"My father rants and raves about minding my own business. My mother tells him not to yell at me."

He rose from the bench. He scanned the area, drew a deep breath and said goodbye. Before he went far, he turned and asked, "Jimmy Byrne is truly Lola's father? It's not just gossip?"

"Yes, unfortunately he is. She wants nothing to do with him, had no idea all these years, and has finally come to terms with it. Lola's a wonderful person. She doesn't have a mean bone in her body and fakes her bravery for the most part."

He nodded and left me sitting alone in the peace and tranquility of the labyrinth. Glad we'd spoken, I waited a while, walked the labyrinth once more, and then went back to the house.

Lola's car had rolled to a stop in the driveway as I walked into the yard. She pulled bags of groceries from the back seat and handed them to me when I came abreast of her.

"Take these and I'll get the other two," she said.

"Are we having company?" I asked eyeing the goods in the bags I carried.

"Aaron and Marcus are coming for lunch and Nana needed several items for her cupboards. Why?"

"When I was at the labyrinth, Martin came by. He said we could leave the island if we wanted to."

She gave me a look of disbelief and then slowed her pace. Softly, Lola said, "I want to find out why these thugs wanted me. I also want to see Jack as soon as possible, but I need to investigate before I leave Block Island." She leaned close and whispered, "Don't tell Nana."

I could feel my eyes widen and my brows hike a bit. "O-okay."

She gave me a nod of finality and marched into the house with me right behind her.

Nana was out and about with her knitting group, honestly, the woman belonged to every group imaginable, and I smiled when Lola read the note she'd left us.

"Your grandmother is busier than a mad hatter. She's always on the go, that must be why she remains so energetic."

"Let's get lunch started and you can tell me about Dave Martin's decision to let us leave."

I washed and cut vegetables, put them in a salad bowl, and sprinkled salt and pepper over the mixture before placing a lid over the salad and refrigerating it. Lola put pieces of chicken in a deep dish, blended spices with oil and vinegar and poured it over the chicken to marinate for a while in the fridge. The sweet smell of fresh basil, garlic, and a few other things she had tossed into the bowl made my mouth water.

We chatted about a trip to the mainland as we worked. I'd been avoiding the subject of the foiled attempt to kidnap her the night before. I shuddered at the memory of being taken without warning. Since I'd walked in those shoes, I knew it was terrifying. I wondered how Lola would deal with it. Would she fall apart, or would she become Little Miss Dynamite, and hold her own against the kidnappers? I shook my head over that thought and said, "You must have been scared when those two goons grabbed you."

"At first, I didn't realize what was happening until they started to drag me a few feet away. That's when Jack flew into action, and you know the rest. I will say that I scratched the daylights out of one of those men. It's likely he'll wear that as a battle scar."

I gave her a keen look. "You didn't say that last night. Did you clean under your fingernails and save any skin tissue that might have gotten stuck in there?"

"Um, no, I didn't, sorry."

I sighed. "Too bad, if this guy was found, the tissue sample could have been tested for a match."

"You know all that legal stuff, Vin. I bake and cook. I don't get involved with that sort of thing. At least, I never used to."

"Haven't you ever watched *Law & Order*, or *NCIS*?" I asked with a chuckle.

"No. I like comedies and competition dance shows." Lola went to the fridge, took out the marinated chicken and asked me to start the grill.

We'd finished setting the table just as Aaron and Marcus arrived. "Perfect timing."

The two men came in, took a seat, and dug into the food as if they'd not eaten in a week, which was a tribute to Lola's cooking. I sneaked the last sliver of chicken off Aaron's plate while he poured iced tea into his glass.

"Did you just steal my food?" His brows were up and his eyes danced with humor.

"It was a mere bite of chicken. You don't care, admit it."

As the meal ended, so did the levity. They'd come with a purpose in mind, cadged a free meal, and now would likely spoil our day. It was annoying to always be right about these things.

Finished with his meal and leaning back in his chair, Aaron asked, "Lola, are you sure you don't know who those men were? Did you get a look at them, any scars, unusual marks or tattoos, anything of that sort?"

With a quick glance at me, Lola mulled over her answer for a second or two. "I might have clawed one of them when I tried to stop their attack on Jack."

He sat back, exchanged looks with Marcus, and then tipped his head to the side. "You didn't tell me that last night. On his face or neck? Where exactly, do you know?"

"Actually, I can't remember, it all happened so fast. I think I got him good though, because he swore. As far as telling you about that last night, I was pretty rattled over the entire event." Lola sighed and then said dryly, "Unlike you three, I live a peaceful life, or I have, until recently."

She slid her chair back and asked sweetly, "Coffee anyone?"

I laughed out loud and got confused looks from Marcus and Aaron. Yeah, they wouldn't understand that I found humor in her peaceful life jibe. Especially, since they hadn't been living in close quarters with her during these difficult times, when she flipped from rough and tough, to the sweet Lola we were all acquainted with. I nodded and said coffee sounded perfect.

His chiseled featured hardened as Marcus asked, "You find this funny, Lavinia?"

"Please, spare me the Lavinia thing. You only use that name when I'm in trouble, and I shouldn't be. Besides, I've done nothing to deserve that attitude. That said, I have a question for you, why didn't either of you mention some of the mobsters are staying in island hotels?"

Lips clamped tight, neither man offered an excuse.

I sweetly, but sarcastically remarked, "Secrets, you do keep secrets, so many of them. I wasn't surprised when I learned that little fact. It's what I've come to expect from both of you. Just know that turnabout is fair play. If you'll excuse me, I have work to do."

I left them sitting with Lola, who could deal with them on her own. She was up to it, and we both knew it. Student materials and a notebook were crammed in a folder on the sideboard, where I'd left it the night before. I grabbed it and headed for the dock.

# Chapter 21

Sometime later, Lola strolled onto the dock, plopped into a chair and stretched out in the sun. I complimented her on the meal, even if the company had turned annoying and judgmental.

In her usual lighthearted way, Lola giggled and admitted I'd caught Aaron and Marcus by surprise when I'd gotten up and walked away. "They wanted to know how you came by the hotel information concerning the mobsters. I had to admit that I didn't know. Glad I didn't have to lie. I'm such a poor liar. Maybe I should practice more."

"Please don't. Lies come back and bite you in the butt, believe me. It was Martin who told me."

"Did he? Why, I wonder?"

"I think he wanted to see my reaction. I explained that though we've been seen with the mob, we hadn't gone willingly. He took that pretty well."

She laughed again. "It's true in a couple of ways and not so true in others, though, right? We did initiate contact in the beginning."

With a snicker, I said, "Mmm, in the beginning, but not too much after that. I hadn't expected to be walked off this property in the middle of the night by a thug who scared the bejeepers out of me. It was creepy." I shivered and then asked, "Have you decided to go to the hospital to see Jack?"

"I want to, but I'm reluctant to leave you by yourself."

"Don't worry about me, take the ferry and go. I'll be fine, and can't leave right now anyway. And, you can tell me about Jack's progress when you get back."

She didn't say anything, but picked at her fingernails instead.

I noticed her hesitation and wondered what else prevented her from leaving. "There's another reason, isn't there?"

"There have been too many murders. I don't believe one family is responsible, or that only one mobster is to blame. Dembrotti and his buddy worked for a Rhode Island mob, right?"

I gave her a nod.

"Then who killed Santilli, and what family was he involved with?"

I shrugged.

"Okay, then let's talk about Johnny Pacci. He was a mobster in his own right, was from Boston, and might have annoyed or insulted Jimmy somehow. Would Jimmy kill him over a trivial matter, or was it to take over Johnny's territory?" Before I could answer, Lola added, "I watched the Godfather, so I'm aware of these things. I also read Joseph "Joe Bananas" Bonanno's autobiography, *A Man of Honor*."

I must have had a look of disbelief on my face, because Lola told me to close my mouth and she then burst into laughter.

"You've been holding out on me. Even I haven't read that book. I don't need to. Actually, I've had enough personal experience with these idiots to last a lifetime."

"I know times have changed since Joe Bananas was in power, but don't you think they probably still use tried and true methods?"

In a dry tone, I said, "I suppose so, since two dead bodies were thrown overboard so they could sleep with the fishes."

Lola shivered. "That is so disgusting."

"Murder is just that, Lola. There's absolutely nothing pleasant about it."

"I'm not going to the hospital. I'll stay here, and we'll figure out what's going on and why. Marcus and Aaron won't like it, and neither will Martin, but that's too bad. I have a score to settle with those two guys who attacked Jack and tried to kidnap me." She rose from her chair, a determined expression on her face. "Let's pay dear old dad a visit."

I jumped up. My notebook fell onto the deck, and I grabbed Lola's arm as she was about to walk away. "Have you lost your mind?"

Her dark eyes snapped with anger as she said, "Not at all. Are you coming or not?"

"What's your plan?"

She hesitated, stared down at her feet for a few seconds, and then conceded. "I guess I should have a plan." She looked up at me. "Help me make one then, it's the least you can do. I know nothing about this stuff, but you often go off on your own without a plan, don't you?"

"I always play it by ear, you know that. Barging in on Jimmy isn't a good idea, it's a disaster. Why would you want to go see him, anyway?"

"He might be able to answer my questions. That's all."

"You aren't thinking he'd step up and be a father, are you? The man has no idea what a father is supposed to be or do. Don't think for one minute he would defend you, or protect you from those men who would have scooped you up last night. They might even have been his goons."

"I guess that's the brutal truth then, isn't it? You've simply pointed out that you and I will solve this mystery. No one else. You're the one I can count on, Vinnie. I know Marcus and Aaron would come to my aid, but they'd have reasons of their own for doing so. You'll do it because we're friends."

"I'm not trying to dissuade you. I simply want you to think it through and not run off without any idea of what could happen. Thugs and their ilk don't follow the same code we do. They have their own rules, and do what they must to survive."

She looked deflated, exhausted, and somewhat discouraged. Guilty for making her feel so, I put my hand on her shoulder. "Sit down, let's talk this out."

We brainstormed for what seemed like hours, and came up with a scheme or sorts. I knew from experience that things didn't always go the way they were supposed to, but it was the best way I knew to move forward. With no plan, things could go wrong in the blink of an eye.

Satisfied that we'd come up with a reasonable way to achieve our goal of finding out who had killed whom, and the reasons why, we dressed for dinner and offered to take Nana along when she arrived home.

"You girls don't need me tagging along," Nana said.

"You deserve a nice evening out and we might not be on the island for much longer, Nana," I said. "Why not allow us to treat you, and enjoy ourselves at the same time?"

She nodded, changed her clothes, and joined us. We drove to the Atlantic Inn, and were shown to a table after a brief wait. When the waiter arrived with the drinks we'd ordered at the bar, he asked if we were ready to order dinner.

I nodded and ordered grilled steak, Lola chose roasted chicken breast roulade, and Nana requested roasted potato gnocchi. I nearly drooled over the food when it arrived.

Artfully arranged and more than enough to satisfy even the hungriest diner, I moaned over the fresh taste of the sautéed asparagus while Nana enjoyed her gnocchi. Lola's meal looked delightful and she offered to share her warm Savoy cabbage and bacon salad with me. I declined and continued on with my steak.

We chatted about Nana's day and the various groups she belonged to on this small island. "You certainly are busy, Nana," Lola noted.

"I believe in keeping myself occupied so I don't become one of those old people who wither away and die before their time."

"Good for you," I said. "Nonni feels the same way. She's forever doing something or going off on a cruise. She tried taking up golf last year. That didn't work out well, but at least she tried."

Nana laughed. "Smart woman, your grandmother. You stay young if you keep moving."

A man walked toward our table and stared at me long and hard. I recognized him as one of the FBI agents that had worked undercover in a Federal Hill restaurant in Providence, but couldn't remember his name. I'd shared tight quarters with him when he'd hauled me into a closet to avoid a man who was looking for me. He raised a brow as he went to a table of well-dressed men. The clothes alone told me these guys weren't agents as their attire was too expensive for that.

Shortly afterward, I excused myself to visit the ladies room, only to realize he was right behind me.

Once we were out of Lola and Nana's sight, he murmured, "Go onto the porch, will you?"

I veered toward the side door and stepped onto the veranda. He guided me to the farthest end of the porch. "You need to get Lola off the island."

I leaned in close and whispered, "I know, I've been trying all day. She refuses to leave until she finds out who tried to snatch her last night and why. Any ideas on that?"

He shook his head. "Aaron can't seem to get a word out of anyone about it, nor can I. None of these guys I'm with tonight will open up. They have circled-the-wagons, so to speak, and no one is saying anything."

A man and woman walked onto the deck and glanced at us. The devilishly handsome agent wrapped his arms around me, pulled me close, and kissed me. It lasted longer than necessary, but when we parted, I caught the man's grin, and his nod at the agent in front of me. Apparently, his actions had been approved of. He and his lady friend walked on, and I leaned against the porch pillar and smiled. "Smooth, very smooth. I remember the last time we met, and you did the same thing."

Unabashed, he admitted, "'It was a perfect opportunity, don't you think?"

"*Mmm*, but let's not make a habit of it, okay?"

He laughed softly, made no promises, and sent me indoors ahead of him after I'd agreed to stay close to Lola if she was adamant about remaining on the island.

Dessert had arrived at our table when I got back. Lola had ordered for me and though I hadn't wanted another bite of food, it looked too luscious to waste. "What is this?" I asked around a mouthful of deliciousness. I allowed the banana cream, toasted peanut ice cream, and the Dulce de Leche caramel to meld together on my tongue.

"It's Banana Mille Fuille," Lola said and grinned as I bit into the caramelized puff pastry filled with goodness. "I thought you might like it. Nana is having the Lime and Chevre Cheesecake and I've got the dark chocolate ganache. This garden mint ice cream is yummy."

Filled to the brim with good food and wondrous desserts, we ordered coffee to be taken on the veranda. Many chairs were inhabited by those who had dined or were waiting to do so when we chose our seats facing the ocean. Moments later, two men came through the door, looked around, and then nodded to the people inside. Three well-dressed men came out, looked one way and then our way and walked toward us. My heart skipped a beat as they drew near.

"Good evening ladies," the men said as they passed.

We smiled and nodded in response, all three of us fully aware we were in the company of mobsters who sat three or four seats away, withdrew cigars from their inner-jacket pockets, and readied them for smoking.

I leaned toward Lola. "We can't get up and leave, it wouldn't be polite," I whispered. "We'll stay five minutes or so and then leave, okay?"

She nodded, as did Nana. I leaned back, enjoyed the breeze that blew cigar smoke away from us toward the other end of the veranda. I chatted about inconsequential matters, urged Lola to enter the conversation by way of giving her a stern look, and then we listened to Nana talk about the latest knitting project she was working on. About ten minutes later, she feigned a yawn and asked if we could leave, since it was past her bedtime.

"Come on then, I'll get you home," Lola remarked sweetly.

We rose, as did the mobsters. They wished us goodnight, we said the same, and tried to look as though we weren't in a hurry to get away. I was two steps from the stairs when the thin high heel of my shoe caught between the boards on the porch. I stumbled, unceremoniously fell, tumbling down the few last stairs onto the walkway. Unharmed, but embarrassed, I sat up and took stock of my shoe. The spike heel had broken off.

Three men rushed to may aid, making lots of sympathetic noises. One of them whispered to me as he helped me off the ground. "Your father says we are here for you if necessary." He tucked a slip of paper into my hand as I shook his, and then he asked, "Can I walk you to your car?"

Lola took me by the arm. "We're fine, thank you."

"Thanks so much," I said to him before hobbling away with Lola.

Once out of earshot, she let go of my arm and quietly asked, "What was that about?"

"Didn't you see me fall down the stairs?"

"That's not what I meant. What did he whisper to you?"

"Just that he hoped I was all right. Why?"

"I thought he might have threatened you."

"No, he was trying to be helpful, is all."

"You're sure?"

I nodded and assured Lola and Nana that the only bruise I'd suffered was to my ego. We made our way to the car. Once we got home and Nana went to bed, Lola and I got the fire pit started. We sat side-by-side, talking about the evening and speculating about the identity of the strangers.

"It's evident they weren't FBI. Did you notice those handmade Fratelli Borgioli Italian shoes one of them wore? I'd recognize them anywhere. They cost over five-hundred dollars."

"I didn't know you were such a shoe aficionado, Lola," I remarked.

"Well, you recognize anything Armani, don't you? I happen to appreciate handmade Italian shoes and Fratelli Borgioli's are fantastic. His suit was also an Italian, handmade Zegna suit that runs about fourteen hundred dollars."

I gawked at her for a moment and saw the twinkle in her eyes as the firelight danced and reflected off her freckled face. We start to laugh. I asked, "Are you sure?"

"You bet I am. While in college, I dated a guy from a wealthy Italian family. He wore expensive suits and shoes, so naturally, I looked up all the information I could find. It was a matter of curiosity for me, because I always wore clothes off the rack, never top-of-the-line designer clothing."

"Just when I thought I knew everything about you, I learn something new."

A vehicle stopped in the yard. The door *thunked* when it closed. I leaned toward Lola and murmured, "Let's hope this is a friendly visit, I'm not up to a battle right now."

"Me either."

"Can I join you ladies?" Aaron asked.

I motioned to a chair and watched him stretch his legs out and lean back with a sigh. "What a long day."

We both sat up and looked at him in surprise.

"It seems nobody wants to talk about your attack last night. Mouths are clamped so tight you'd think they'd been glued shut." Aaron ran a hand through his hair. He turned his head from side-to-side and rolled his shoulders.

I'd never noticed him show signs of tension. "Frustrated with your friends, are you?"

"I certainly am. Not one person will even discuss the event. Usually, when there's an attempted kidnapping or murder, that's all these guys speculate over. It's sort of dinner table chat between thugs."

I laughed. Lola poked me with her elbow, and I grunted from the jab. When I slanted a look in her direction, she smiled sweetly.

"It's not funny, Vin," she murmured.

"Sorry, but I can't imagine you not being able to get at least one man to open up. Could it be they're afraid of repercussions from Jimmy Byrne if they talk openly?"

"That's possible. It's not clear if Jimmy knows, but I'd bet he does. Could be he's made noise about it, and while he'd do so cautiously, his response would be clear."

"Lola and I were considering a visit with him to discuss the subject. Not that either of us believe he'd come to her aid in a million years, that is. We're merely curious as to what his opinion is over what happened."

"Stay away from him, both of you. This isn't a game, Vinnie."

Lola piped up. "We're aware of that."

Aaron looked at her. "Have you heard how Casella is doing?"

Lola's eyes widened. "Not yet. Why, has he taken a turn for the worse?"

Aaron shook his head. "Not that I know of. As of this afternoon, he was sitting up in bed complaining about the food. Guess it's safe to say he's not critical any longer."

Her sigh was audible and her expression one of relief.

I threw a few sticks of wood on the fire and settled back into my chair. "I told you he would be all right."

"Yeah, I know, but you didn't see how awful he looked after the incident. I think I'll give him a call later."

"Aaron, we can leave the island, though I don't feel that I can until we figure out who tried to abduct Lola, and why, or she won't be safe anywhere."

"I understand your point, I really do. But, to become involved, in what could easily turn deadly, would be a major mistake," Aaron warned. "What does your father think about you and Lola staying here?"

"He's not going to know we can leave if I have my way about it, so keep your mouth shut on that front, will you? And that goes for Marcus, too."

Aaron agreed with a nod and said, "Speaking of Marcus, he broke up a fight between two of Burgatti's men tonight. I haven't any idea what the altercation was about, but they both landed in Martin's holding cells for the night. They may have had too much to drink, and I'm sure Burgatti won't be happy about the unwanted attention."

"Isn't Salvatore Burgatti from one of the New York City crime families?" Lola wanted to know.

Again, I gave her a look of surprise that caused her to laugh softly.

"Vinnie doesn't read the paper like we do, Aaron. She gets her news online."

Before I could protest, Aaron smiled and said, "The feds have been watching Burgatti for some time now, the problem being, they can't catch him in any illegal activities."

Out of the darkness behind us, Marcus said, "Lola, would you come with me please? I'd like you to take a look at one of these men."

I nearly jumped out of my skin when he spoke. We hadn't heard him arrive and it brought memories of Dembrotti's ghost to mind. He popped up whenever he liked, too, without a sound.

"Geez, Marcus, you scared me half to death," I snapped.

"Nervous tonight, Vin?" His brow arched, shadows deepening from the fire dancing across his features.

I shrugged, thought about what had happened earlier in the evening, the message from my father, and remembered the agent who'd kissed me. "You could say that."

# Chapter 22

We climbed into the Yukon and rode in silence to the police station. Before Lola could get out, I touched her arm and whispered, "Be very careful of what you say."

She promised she would, and we went inside to meet with Dave Martin, who seemed less than happy to see us. I offered a smile, but got a stern look in return. So it would be like that, huh? My inner voice popped in. *Give him a break, will you? He's got a crappy job to do. You and the mob have infiltrated his island, and don't you think you'd feel the same as he does, if it were you?*

I heaved a sigh, silently wished the voice would find a new home, and at the same time, I realized that would definitely be the case if I was in Dave Martin's shoes. I waited for Marcus to bring Lola into the holding area and then watched as she came out, her face pasty white, and her dark eyes huge and scared. I reached out and put my arm around her shoulders.

"Come on, let's go outside."

Martin blocked our path and we halted in front of him. I stepped into his space and said, "Get out of our way."

Aaron had remained outside lest he be seen in the presence of the police, by the prisoners, which could bring suspicion to his cover.

Marcus spoke up. "Lavinia."

"What?"

"Dave would like to ask Lola a few questions. She'll be fine, Vinnie."

"Sit over here, Lola," Dave urged kindly.

With a brief glance at me, she nodded and took a seat.

"Did you recognize one of those men?"

"Yes," she murmured.

"You said you didn't get a look at either of them at the time of the incident. How would you recognize him, now?"

"By the scratch on his face and neck." Lola had regained her composure as I stood next to her chair for moral support. Unused to being questioned and harangued by those with power, Lola was a newbie at this game. All said though, I was sure she could handle whatever came her way.

"You're certain?"

"I am."

Martin offered his thanks and looked at Marcus. "Since we have no concrete proof other than that scratch, I don't think I can hold this guy for attempted kidnapping and assault. I can keep him overnight for disturbing the peace. Will that give you the time you need to gather evidence of your own?"

"I can't say for sure, but I'll use any time I can get."

"Keep me posted, Marcus. Thank you for coming in, Lola." Martin turned his attention to me. "As for you, I recommend you keep that temper under control in the future, or you'll be sharing a cell with those two bums."

"I apologize. It's been a rough day. Sorry," I said and walked out the door with Lola in tow.

Lola hurried to keep pace with my long stride. "One of these days you're going to be arrested for abusing an officer of the law."

"I couldn't care less. It irks me when these guys get high and mighty. It's not as if they don't break their own rules. Cripes, you'd think I was a bad person when the island is currently loaded with them." I flipped my hair away from my face and said, "Was he one of the men from last night?"

She nodded. "I think so. I got him good, and his bruises aren't from the fist fight tonight, they look too old. I think Jack got in a few punches of his own before they overwhelmed him."

By this time, we'd reached Aaron's SUV and saw him leaning against it with his arms folded. Marcus came up behind us. "I'll leave you here and walk back to the marina. Trooper Maddox is waiting for me. I'll come by in the morning to pick up my motorcycle. Vinnie, can I see you for a minute?"

Grudgingly, I walked over to him.

In a soft voice, he said, "I understand you feel you must protect Lola, but we only want to help her. Causing hard feelings with Martin won't be good for you should you end up in a bind. He's right. You need to keep your temper under control."

"I know. I'll try. I'd just like to go home and forget all this, you know? One minute Martin is nice and the next he's rude and threatening. We both know how I get when threatened."

"Why don't you and Lola go back to the mainland?"

"If we go before her would-be kidnappers are found, she'll never be safe. At least here she can't go too far without someone noticing."

His arms folded, Marcus gave me a questioning look. "Tell me you aren't planning to investigate on your own."

"Not if I have any say in it. Lola wanted to go talk to Jimmy Byrne today. I stopped her before she could. We almost had an argument, which would be a first in our friendship. Her determination can be daunting."

He started to laugh and then said, "She is Little Miss Dynamite, you know."

I smiled, and said I'd stay in touch.

"Do that, I'll work on finding out who tried to snatch her," he said as I walked back to the SUV.

We rode to the house. Aaron dropped us off, and Lola and I went inside. I figured it had been a long day for all of us. We plopped into our favorite chairs in the sunroom and sipped wine that Lola had brought in from the kitchen.

"What do you think we should do, Vin?"

"Let's just kick-back and relax for a few days. If nothing happens, we'll go home."

"Sounds good to me. What did Marcus say?"

To keep my temper in hand, and then he mentioned we should go home."

"And you said?"

"That you won't be safe until the men who tried to kidnap you are apprehended. He took it well, and said he'll work on it."

Lost in our own thoughts, we sat quietly for a while. I yawned, she giggled and did the same and then got up to head to bed. The sound of breaking glass brought us around and we raced from the house into the yard.

The rear window of Lola's Cooper was shattered. Carefully, we walked toward the car when things went wild.

I glimpsed Lola being lifted off her feet as a cloth hood was pulled down over my head. My arms were held tightly behind my back. I kicked and bumped against the man as another secured ropes at my wrists. His grunts were loud enough for me to know I had hurt him. I kicked out again, and again, listening for Lola who hadn't made a sound. When I finally connected with another body, I was shoved to the ground, then harshly told to shut up and stay where I was or I'd wish I had.

Smart enough to know better than to push my luck, I lay silent on the shell-paved driveway, listening intently to the muffled voices that floated on the breeze.

"Get in the car, this one won't be a problem."

A car door slammed shut and sped away. I remained immobile for a bit for fear someone had stayed behind, then I struggled into a sitting position. With difficulty, I forced my body to relax and slid my hands down under my butt to free my arms and bring them forward. Wrists bound, my hands still worked so I ripped the hood off my head. I chewed at the knots to loosen them. Once loose, I spread my wrists to stretch the rope enough to slip a hand out. All the while, I wondered why Nana hadn't heard the noise, but figured maybe she'd had too much to drink, and was snoring soundly.

I pulled my cell phone from my pocket and dialed the phone number on the slip of paper given to me earlier. A voice answered on the first ring. Worried, tears of anger flowed down my face. I said Lola had been taken.

"I'll pick you up. Wait outside." He hung up.

I stuffed the phone into my pocket, then thought better of it and called my father.

"It's after midnight, what's wrong?"

Amid my tears, I told him Lola had been abducted.

"Lavinia, did you call the number that was given to you at the restaurant tonight?"

"Y—yeah."

"Then wait. You'll have help in a minute or so. I'll talk to you soon." He hung up. I shook the phone, and swore as I tucked it into my pocket.

A car slowed at the end of the driveway. The headlights flashed once, and I ran toward it. The driver's side window slowly descended and a dark-eyed, dark-haired man told me to get in. Frantic, I ran to the passenger side and scrambled into the car. No fear, no ranting of my inner voice about the hazards of being foolish, nothing. I just did as I was instructed.

"What happened?" He asked as we drove toward the marina.

"Your name is?" I asked before answering him.

"Blake."

Funny, he didn't look like a Blake, but who knew what his mother was thinking when she named this handsome, dark Italian. His bad boy looks were breath-taking. "O-okay, Blake, we heard glass breaking, went to see what had happened, and were jumped. Lola was dragged off. My wrists were tied, and a hood was pulled over my head. I struggled with the man or men who bound me and got a couple good kicks in before being thrown to the ground and threatened. They have Lola, and I have no idea who took her, or where." Fear burned in my gut and *Vengeance* sat chipmunk-like on my shoulder, encouraging me to conjure up ways in which to make Lola's abductors pay for taking her.

Blake was calm, too calm for comfort. His was a scary kind of calm.

We rolled to a stop at the far end of the pier. Blake parked and shut down the motor. "Let's go."

"Where?"

"Just come with me. It'll be okay, I'm a good guy, honest."

Yeah, like I believed that for a New York second. But then, what choice did I have? I had called him in the first place. My father had better know what he was doing by sending this man to help me.

I followed him to a yacht, just beyond several others, and felt salty wind on my face. Everything was quiet as we walked along the dimly lit dock. My wrists smarted from rope burns, and would be raw for a few days from having struggled against the rough binding, though that was the least of my problems. We stepped onto the yacht, were met by two men I recognized from dinner, and I listened as Blake spoke Italian to them.

"Abbiamo problemi. Ottenere questa donna un drink e portarci al boss."

He'd said there was a problem and that I should have a drink. Okay, I'd understood that much, but was unsure of what more I'd gather if he spoke too quickly. His dialect was different than that of my parents, which made it a tad difficult to understand all that was said.

One man left to get the drink, or that's what I assumed, anyway. The other beckoned us to follow him. I worried about where.

The second man stopped outside the double doors and asked, "Dove si trova la piccola donna?"

I guessed he wanted to know where Lola was. I held my breath as Blake looked at me and then said, "Penso che lei è stata presa da Burgatti."

He thought Burgatti had her? Why? Why would a crime family from New York want Jimmy's daughter? Silent, I never let on I understood. It served my purposes for the moment and might come in handy later.

With a knock on the door, we summoned to enter. The man carrying my drink walked in behind us, and once inside the salon, handed me a glass of amber liquid. I sniffed it, downed the whiskey in one gulp, choked on the strength of it, and then told him thank you. I received a smile in return. My nerves came back to life. My fear fled, and the anger in my gut simmered. *Vengeance* was back, sitting on my shoulder, incessantly chattering in my ear. I drew a breath, wishing *Vengeance* would shut up.

I handed the glass to the man who'd brought it, and turned to face my host. He and two of the other men, along with Blake, had been part of the crew dining at the inn earlier. Still not knowing my host's name, what his connection was to my father, or why he'd agreed to help Lola and me, I gave him what I hoped was a confident smile and said, "Hello."

He offered a slight smile. His teeth were so white, they fairly gleamed. "Ms. Esposito, it's nice to finally have the chance to speak with you. Our brief meeting earlier wasn't a good time for either of us. Come, sit down, I want to introduce you to the family."

I gave Blake a glance, he offered a slight nod and watched as I ventured forth to sit in one of the chairs clustered near the man I knew for certain was a mafia don. I reached out and shook his hand when he offered his. The others in the room made no move to take a seat.

I tipped my head toward them and whispered, "They're making me nervous."

His eyes lit with laughter, he summoned the goons and Blake to relax and sit with us. I expected guards outside the door, and concluded we were safe, even if only for the moment.

My host introduced himself as Alessio Quatrini, head of the Haven, Connecticut family.

"This is my nephew, Amerigo Pesti, my sister's boy, and this man Dante Romano, is my half-brother's son. Of course, you already know Blake Benedetto. We aren't related, however, his father was my consigliere until he died from a heart attack several years ago. Blake has taken his place."

Aware of the role Blake played as a consigliere, I raised my brows a tad and looked at him. Unlike in the movies, in real-life, a mafia consigliere is generally the number three person in a crime family, after the boss and underboss[1] in most cases. It's no small position to hold and trust has to be profound to become part of this three-man ruling panel. Blake was one of the few in the crime family who could argue with the boss, and would often be tasked with challenging him when needed, to ensure subsequent plans were foolproof. I didn't envy Blake, but my gut told me he did it well, which begged the question of the family's relationship with my father.

I nodded to each man in turn and then thanked Quatrini for having me aboard.

He inclined his head and said, "You must be wondering why I'm willing to help you, Ms. Esposito?"

"Lavinia, please. Yes, it's the question I've been asking myself since I saw you at the inn."

His smile warmed a bit. He had thick, bushy eyebrows, a strong, jutting jaw, high cheekbones, and eyes as blue as the sea. Surely his heritage came from Northern Italy, where many Italians were blue-eyed.

"Your friend, Lola, has been kidnapped by Burgatti's men. He knows she's the daughter of Jimmy Byrne, a no-good criminal if ever there was one. I'm sure Burgatti plans to use her to negotiate for Jimmy's territory, or part of it. I don't believe Burgatti has thought

---

1. http://www.wow.com/wiki/Underboss?s_pt=aolsem&s_chn=14

things through, though. We know that Jimmy won't negotiate when it comes to losing his power and income. In fact, he won't give a fig if Lola is killed."

My heart pounded against my ribs. Quatrini was right. Byrne didn't care about anyone, but himself. I leaned forward a bit and stared into those deep blue eyes. "Why are you interested in this?"

"If Burgatti takes a hold in Boston, it will be bad for my business. Besides, I owe your father a favor."

"Oh, well, I appreciate the help. What's your plan?"

"Nothing you need to know about. You can't be held responsible for what happens if you aren't aware of what will take place."

"I don't mean any disrespect, or want to seem argumentative, but I would like to be part of those who will rescue Lola. She must be out of her mind with fear. I can't let Burgatti, or anyone else, harm her. You do understand that, don't you?"

He smiled, said my father had intimated that I would insist on being involved in Lola's rescue, and said, "I promised Gino no harm would come to you, and that's my stand on the matter. I hope you won't try to interfere, Lavinia."

My mind was hard at work on how, when, and where the rescue would take place. Would it be on open seas where only the coast guard could board them? Would Quatrini send his men to Burgatti's yacht and take her from them while in port? Was Burgatti on a yacht? I didn't have a clue.

Men—you can't deal with them and you can't kill them, so I guessed I'd simply have to agree and do my own thing. I agreed to leave him to his plan, but had my toes crossed all the while. If I could help Lola, then I would, no matter what anyone said.

"Do you know where she's being held?"

"She's in a house on the island that's well guarded." He raised his hand and said, "That's all I'll say, so don't ask which one."

"Okay, I just wondered." I glanced at the clock on the wall and said, "I should get back to the house. If Lola's grandmother finds us both gone, there will be an uproar the likes of which I've probably never seen."

"Blake will take you back. Say nothing of this to anyone. Nothing, understand?"

"I do, thank you for helping us. I appreciate it." I didn't believe for one moment it was a promise I could keep.

We left and drove back to the house. Blake parked just before the driveway and said, "You'll be fine, and so will Lola. I promise, Vinnie."

I gave him a long hard stare and asked, "How do you know my father?"

"Rudy Santilli was my uncle. Goodnight." He reached across me and opened the door.

"Goodnight. *Umm*, I was very sorry to hear of Rudy's passing."

He gave me an unfathomable look and then nodded. I closed the door, stepped back, and motioned him on. The car's motor purred like a slumbering lion as he drove away. I watched until the taillights disappeared and then walked into the yard. The house was dark, no light shone from the windows other than a tiny lamp in the kitchen. I might have stumbled if the moon hadn't been bright. This nocturnal stuff was ridiculous.

Once inside, I listened for signs of Nana being awake. Nothing. Not a peep from upstairs.

A glass of wine in my hand, I sat in the living room with only the brightness of the moon to keep me company. My mind went round and round until I came up with an idea.

???

Nana shook my shoulder. I opened my eyes and saw her gazing down at me. "Where's Lola this morning, and what are you doing here in the living room?"

"I couldn't sleep and ended up having a late night. Lola isn't up yet?" I got off the sofa and trudged toward the staircase.

With a shake of her head, Nana said, "I'll start the coffee while you get her out of bed."

"Sure," I said, and wondered how this would play out. Lies, lies, and more lies. Good grief, I was sick of them. Reaching the upstairs landing, my cell phone rang. My father was on the line.

"How did things work out last night?"

"Fine, I promised to keep my nose out of it, which should make you very happy," I murmured.

"Good." He hung up, and I tucked my phone in my pocket.

I counted to ten, then headed back downstairs. Entering the kitchen, I said, "Lola isn't in her room. Her bed is made, too."

"I didn't hear her go out, did you?"

I shook my head as I poured a cup of coffee for each of us. "Maybe she went to the market early or something. Did you look to see if she was on the dock?" I asked innocently.

She peered out the window and then shook her head. "This isn't like her at all. Do you think she left on the early morning ferry? I know she said she wanted to visit Jack at the hospital."

I shrugged and said she had mentioned that, but hadn't said she was going today. How would I explain the damage to Lola's car window? I took a swig of coffee and turned to the petite woman whose face held a bit of worry.

"I'll go look outside, maybe she went to the labyrinth. I've been talking about it for days and she seemed interested." I put my cup on the table and walked outside before Nana could say a word.

I stopped at the car, slowly assessed the damage and then rushed indoors. "Call the police, I think Lola is missing. Her rear car window has been smashed. I think she's gone."

Fast to act, Nana dialed Martin and ordered him to come to the house.

Within minutes, Dave Martin strode into the room. "Would you like to tell me what happened to Lola's car?"

His eyes snapped with anger, and his features were stiff and hard. Clearly, he'd brook no foolishness today.

"I'd say someone smashed the window."

"Apparently, but there's more to it, isn't there?"

I refused to cave in to his stern attitude, even if he took me to a holding cell. I had promised to stay out of Alessio Quatrini's business, and to say something now would only raise an alarm that could bring Aaron and Marcus to my door.

"If I knew where Lola was, I'd tell you. I'm worried sick over it, and that's the truth. That's why I had Nana call you in the first place. We'll help in any way we can. You know this island inside and out. Where do you think she could be?"

"Was anyone upset with her?"

Nana and I shook our heads.

"Did she go to the mainland?"

"I doubt it. She'd have told us she was going."

"When did you see her last?"

"The three of us had dinner last night. Nana went to bed when we got home, and I fell asleep on the sofa in the living room. I didn't hear a thing. We've looked everywhere for her on the property." So much for helping out and being truthful.

He gave me a cold look of disbelief and walked outside, talked into his radio, and waited a moment as he received an answer. In an instant, he came back inside. Nana and I waited for the next round of questions.

"The other officers have been dispatched to ride the island and check locations out. I will ask Marcus and Maddox to question those onboard the yachts and boats. There aren't enough officers to go around." Martin stepped past me and stood in front of Nana, he promised they would do their best to bring Lola home.

After Martin had driven away to coordinate the search, Nana said, "He'll be as useless as a fart in the wind. What can I do to help you find my granddaughter?"

"First we'll have breakfast, then we'll come up with ideas of where she could be."

Nana and I had a simple breakfast consisting of fresh fruit and bowls of cereal. I smiled when I remembered the fare we'd had with Lola every morning, then I sobered, thinking of where she was and how she was being treated.

"Are there many empty homes on the island at this time of year?" I asked.

"No, usually owners rent out their homes to help defray the costs of owning here. I'll call Cora. She knows everything that goes on. I'll ask which houses are empty. You wait one minute."

Nana picked up the phone, got a pad and pencil and dialed Cora's number. They chatted for a bit before Nana popped the question. I watched her tuck the phone between her chin and shoulder and scribble furiously on the pad.

"You said there is another house you're unsure of?" Nana asked and listened. Again, she jotted down the information that was given and made the excuse that I loved the island so much, I wanted to rent a house for the remainder of the month. She then said goodbye. Smooth, the woman was smooth.

Nana ripped the page from the notebook and handed it to me while pointing to the first two addresses. "These are the places that are empty, and Cora isn't sure about this one."

I nodded, thanked her, and tucked the paper into the pocket of my cropped pants. "I'm going into the village to rent a Moped. If Marcus comes by for his motorcycle, don't mention where I've gone, or he'll call out the National Guard for sure."

"You go get my girl, Vinnie. If you need a gun, I have my husband's handgun upstairs."

I shied away from her offer. "No guns, they're too dangerous. Besides, I don't know how to shoot."

"You can't shoot it. I don't have any bullets. All you need it for, is to show you mean business."

"No, Nana, really, I'll manage." I rushed out the door, scurried down the road and onto the main drag to stop at the scooter rental place. Usually there were two or three open in full season. Today was such a day. Fearful the young woman at the rental stand that I'd used before would refuse me, I chose a different one.

I stepped up and asked for the tan Moped on the left. The kid handling the deals took my money, handed over the keys and said "Don't wreck it, okay?"

I smiled, promised I'd bring it back in one piece, and asked for a map of the island's roads. He handed me a tourist's pamphlet and I took off.

# Chapter 23

Traffic was nil, the day gorgeously bright, the sky blue, and if I hadn't any worries, I'd have taken delight in my ride. Instead, I was on the lookout for potential gangsters, thugs, hoodlums, and that sort of no-good fiend.

The first address was Clay Head Trail. I rode as far in as I could, parked the Moped, and walked part of the trail. Ten minutes in, I knew I wouldn't find Lola there, and turned back. Nothing appeared suspicious so I drove onto Corn Neck Road and went toward the next place on Nana's list.

At Beacon Hill Road, I took a left. The unpaved road jostled me, nearly sent me flying a couple of times and might even have loosened a tooth or two when I hit a deep pot hole, but I had a mission and wouldn't be deterred from it. Again, I came up empty-handed. My angst was growing by the minute. It would never do to accept defeat. It wasn't in my genes to do so, which meant the only thing I could do was try the third address.

I slowed the Moped to a stop once I'd reached Dorry's Cove. I parked on the side of the road, crept to the tall hedges, and heard two men arguing about the sweet cottage and the lack of entertainment on the island.

"Criminy, we're stuck here babysitting that redhead who is making my life miserable. You can tell she's related to Byrne, that's for sure."

The second man chimed in. "She sure can cook, though."

"Yeah, I'll give her that. Too bad she's so miserable. It's not as if we're being mean."

I smiled, knew Little Miss Dynamite was just fine, and figured I'd come back after dark. I'd have to turn the Moped in by sundown. Lola's car was drivable, since only the rear window had been damaged in order to get our attention. I ran toward the Moped, rolled it down the road, and then got on, raced back into town, and returned it to the rental stand.

The kid thanked me for not destroying it. I guessed he knew who I was, and that must be due to gossip flowing quickly between the islanders. I smiled, handed him the key, and sauntered off. I walked the beach, sat in the sun for a bit and enjoyed the wind and salty air. I considered how I'd get Lola out of the house, when a voice from behind startled me.

"I'm surprised to see you on the beach, Vin." Aaron hunkered down beside me.

"I needed to get away from the house. Nana is upset, and rightly so."

"I just came from there. She's very worried, and if I were in her shoes, I'd feel the same way. Instead, I'm worried about you and Lola. I know you've been riding around the island on a Moped. You've been looking for her, haven't you?"

"I have. My father warned me to stay out of the search, but I can't leave this to the authorities."

His features stiffened as he exclaimed, "Christ, Vinnie, you're such a loose cannon. Let the police do their job, will you?"

Leaning in close, I said, "I wouldn't let Dave Martin walk my dog, let alone have faith enough that he could rescue Lola."

He snorted. "You don't have a dog."

"No, but I have Lola. Do you honestly think that man can save her?"

He stared out over the ocean as waves rolled on and away from the sand, leaving a wet path in their wake. "Probably not. His station is unequipped for this sort of event and all else that's been going on these past weeks."

I held a tiny snail shell in my palm, rolled it back and forth, and thoughtfully ran my fingertips over its ridges. I gazed at it, then at Aaron.

"What are you doing to help in the matter?"

"My job is to keep peace in the families, nothing more. I have my orders, Vin, sorry."

"You are such a liar, Aaron Grant. Do not expect me to believe you wouldn't move heaven and earth to find Lola."

His warm brown eyes regarded me, and he gave a slight smile. "You're right. Why did I think I could get that lie by you? I have feelers out as to where she's been taken, and if she's all right. Did you come up with anything concrete in your travels over the island?"

Staring out over the water, I shook my head and sighed. "If I get my hands on those men who have Lola, they will be very sorry."

"Okay, say you find them. What would you do?"

"Play it by ear, like I always do. Why?"

"We could play it by ear together."

I turned and poked him with my elbow. "Don't give me that, you're trying to trap me into telling you what I saw on my little jaunt."

"I know you found something. And by the way, why didn't you call me last night when she was abducted?"

"I couldn't. Sorry."

He stood, brushed the sand off his trousers, and hauled me to my feet. "Lavinia Esposito, you drive me crazy. It's clear you're not telling me what you know. I can't be of use to you if I'm in the dark, so speak up, or I'll have Martin toss you in jail."

I gave him a shove, sent him stumbling back a few steps, and then warned, "Don't ever threaten me, not ever. I'm not an idiot, nor am I stupid. At this moment, I don't have much confidence in law enforcement's ability to find Lola, so back off."

"May I remind you that I saved you from your kidnappers?"

"You did, but there weren't all these mafia people hanging about on yachts and in hotels. My situation was much different than this one. If whoever took Lola wants to bargain with her dear-old-dad, then he's quite mistaken. Jimmy cares only for himself and his own interests."

"You're right about that." He placed his hands on my arms and drew me close. "I know you're afraid Lola will be harmed, so let's work together to find her. Come on, I'll buy you lunch."

Never willing to miss a chance to eat, I agreed. We walked off the beach, entered a restaurant and ordered beer and salads.

"Tell me what you found, and how you found it," Aaron urged softly as his glance took in everyone in the place. Our panoramic view was from a far corner table.

Why I put my trust in this man, I couldn't say, I simply did and hoped I wasn't foolhardy in doing so. Postponing the inevitable confession, which Aaron seemed to draw out of me on many an occasion, I asked, "Have some of the families returned home? The marina looks a tad empty."

He swallowed a mouthful of beer and nodded. "Many have left. They concluded their summit meeting, and will now implement whatever it is they've agreed upon. Only a couple of *businessmen* remain. Why?"

I snickered at the term. My aunt always called her racketeer boyfriend a *businessman*, which tickled me to no end, and annoyed my parents beyond reason, especially my father.

"I see. In other words, only the ones who can't iron out their business agreements are still here?"

He inclined his head, munched his salad, and around a mouthful of food, Aaron said, "Don't sidestep, Lavinia."

"What are you doing tonight?"

He sat back, fiddled with his beer bottle label and then smiled.

"I think we should take a ride to Dorry's Cove Road later," I said softly.

"Really?"

"Are you in?"

He nodded. "What time would you like to go?"

"At nightfall. If you tell anyone, I will kick your butt. Doing this alone is dangerous, and I certainly can't take Nana, even if she is formidable."

He smiled and agreed. "She can be. I've noticed you don't pull any stunts around her. When she asks a question you work hard to not lie. Proud of you for that, Vin. Nana's a great woman."

We finished our meal. I drank the rest of my beer, and said I had to get back to Nana's.

"Let me drop you off. I'll feel better knowing you aren't on foot and vulnerable. At the rate things are going, who knows what'll happen next."

We climbed into the Yukon. "You never said how you found her."

"Nana gave me a list of houses that might not have been rented for the summer. I didn't have any luck with the first two addresses, but hit pay-dirt on the third."

"You saw Lola?"

I thought of the conversation between Lola's guards.

"There were two guys outside the house. One of them whined over how boring the island was, and that they had to babysit the temperamental redhead. The other guy said she was a fabulous cook, though, and that's when I knew they had Lola. Little Miss Dynamite is in action, and someone will pay for taking her."

He turned into the driveway. "I'll see you at sundown. Wear dark clothes, and be ready."

"I will."

? ? ?

The screen door closed behind me as I walked through the short hallway and into the kitchen. Nana had two tall glasses of iced tea on the table when I entered the room. Lemon wedges bobbed invitingly in each glass.

"I didn't tell Aaron anything." She raised her hand and crossed her heart as she handed me a glass.

"I know, he said as much. I think he and Marcus, as well as Dave Martin, are afraid of you, Nana."

"Pshaw, if they only knew what a pushover I am."

I smiled and thought she might not have considered how intimidating she could seem.

"Good news."

Her eyes lit up. "You found her?"

"I did. She'll be rescued tonight. It isn't safe to try anything in the daylight. I'll have to wait until darkness falls."

She jumped from her chair, ran to mine, and hugged me with all her might. I struggled to breathe and said, "Aaron will come with me. I'll need that handgun, Nana, just for show."

"Anything you want. Anything at all." Nana hurried from the room, up the stairs, and then brought down the deadliest looking 9mm Sig Sauer I'd ever laid eyes on. I was no gun enthusiast, so any weapon scared the bejeepers out of me, but this one instantly brought on the willies.

Nana slapped the gun down in front of me. "Here you go. Like I said, no bullets, no shooting. For looks only."

I reached out, ran my index fingertip over the barrel and handgrip, and then shivered. I pushed it away and shook my head. "I think I've changed my mind."

"Don't be silly, those men holding Lola must have guns. If you plan to scoop her from under their noses, you should have a weapon to look as threatening as they will." She pushed the gun back in my direction.

"O—okay then." I gulped the tea, wished it was whiskey, and almost said so. Dutch courage was better than no courage, right?

We hung about for the rest of the day, Nana talking about her life on Block Island and my attention as rapt as it could be under the circumstances. She went on about the snow storms in the early years, and how children slid down the roads on thick pieces of cardboard, enjoying the freeness of it all. I smiled as she gave accounts of what life was like back in the day, so different from now. So many folks didn't live on Block Island all year round, but that had changed, as had life. In fact, she said true islanders looked forward to the end of tourist season. Life became quiet and serene without the hubbub tourists brought.

We had a light supper around six-thirty, and I sat outside on the dock awaiting nightfall. As the sun dipped lower and lower, I went inside and donned dark jeans, a black jersey, my navy blue hooded sweatshirt, and sneakers. I tucked the alarming weapon in my waistband, and pulled the sweatshirt down over it to keep it hidden.

The Yukon pulled into the driveway, I told Nana not to worry, and I went off to bring Lola home.

We drove part of the way down Dorry's Cove Road before Aaron pulled the huge SUV into a cropping of bushes. From there, we went the rest of the way on foot. The moon was waning; light from it wasn't as bright as it had been, though the stars that dotted the sky were incredible. I tripped and stumbled a couple of times until Aaron finally took my hand and guided me along.

Our approach to the house wasn't as clear as I'd thought it would be. Day and night brought different views of things. Stone walls lined the road for a bit, then tall, nicely pruned bushes took over from there. Lights from the house were low, people could be seen moving about and we crept up the lawn to the side of the house.

Crouched under the open windows, we listened.

"This meal is terrific. I wish we could keep you."

"Consider this your last supper, boys. I go on strike tomorrow." Her remark brought a grin to my lips and I almost laughed aloud. Lola wasn't afraid, or was acting like she wasn't, anyway. Instead, she'd done what she did best, she'd found her way into their hearts by feeding them. I was sure her Julia Roberts smile had been useful in the melting process as well. No man could resist it. I glanced at Aaron and saw his smile, the shake of his head, and then we heard cars arrive.

Fear gripped my gut. I couldn't move, and Aaron fairly dragged me away from our hiding spot as men surrounded the house. We'd reached the edge of the bushes where shadows were deep and we couldn't be seen.

Whispers drifted on the ever-constant breeze. "Take her. Remove anyone who gets in your way. She's not to be harmed, understand?"

"Will do." The men spread out like peanut butter on bread, thinning slightly, yet knowing where to go and what to do.

I shrank back into the bush behind me and felt Aaron do the same. Neither of us were small, so hiding wasn't as easy as it would be for Little Miss Dynamite.

Surprised voices rang out. Men were yelling, and then I heard Lola's voice. "It's about damn time someone came for me."

I heard his voice, shook my head, and then swallowed hard. "Aaron, let's get out of here."

"No, Vinnie, I think not. We'll wait right here."

"We have to leave, right now."

"Why?"

"Because, just because." I moved out of the shrubs, ran as fast as my legs would take me, and hurtled over the stone wall. Long legs do come in handy.

Aaron followed suit and we fled to his Yukon.

Once inside the truck, my chest heaved until I caught my breath. Oh great, my father had come to rescue Lola. I was in a mind-boggled state and had no idea what to think or do. All I knew was that my dad had come out of nowhere. Men had followed orders, and he had rescued my best friend.

"You're shaking, are you okay?"

I nodded and wrapped my arms as far around my torso as they would stretch.

"Was that your father's voice I heard?"

I shrugged and muttered, "It would seem so."

He laughed, truly laughed, and then said, "Well, what do you know ——"

The motor was running. We backed out of our hiding place and drove to Nana's. A half hour later, Lola was delivered to the door by Blake and his cronies. Lola hugged all of us in turn while Blake stared at me and then tipped his head for me to join him.

I sidled from the room, while Aaron had his back to me, and met Blake on the dark side of the house.

"Where's my father?"

"I have no idea what you're talking about."

"Fine, then what do you want?"

"Tell me, what were you doing there? You promised to stay out of it."

"No, I said I wouldn't interfere with your plan. I kept my word. I didn't interfere."

"Semantics," Blake said.

"Indeed," I remarked.

He leaned in, gave me a quick kiss, and took his leave.

Dumbfounded, I leaned against the house. Suddenly, I realized I'd been blindsided by the kiss, so there'd be no confrontation over my father. Maybe I was better off not being told he was truly there, though Dad and I would have words when I got home.

A few moments later, I heard Aaron call my name. I went to meet him as he asked what I was doing outside.

"Just thanking my lucky stars, I guess. It's amazing that Lola was rescued under our noses. I'm not sure we could have pulled it off between the two of us."

"It could have gotten a bit more complicated than it turned out to be. She's back now, and that's all that matters." His cell phone jingled, and he stepped away to answer it. He listened, said he'd be right there, and then left.

I hugged the daylights out of Lola, and told her how glad I was to see her safe. "Aaron and I were outside the window listening to you tell those men it was their last supper. I guess you were right, huh?"

"I didn't know you were there until Nana told me a few minutes ago. I knew you'd rescue me if you could."

"It was all I could do to stay away this afternoon, but I didn't know how many guards were on the premises. I confessed to Aaron that I knew where you were, and we hatched a plan for tonight. I should have known Quatrini's men would beat us to it. They did say they were prepared to extricate you." I leaned forward and whispered, "Nana doesn't know you were taken last night. Watch what you say, okay?"

Lola nodded. "Let's break out the wine and celebrate, shall we?"

"Count me in."

Nana joined us in the living room. We listened to how Lola had been taken to the house, then she'd offered to make a meal for the men if they would buy the ingredients, and since they were so hungry, they gave in. One thug was sent to the market to shop. I laughed at her guile, and knew our worry was for naught. Little Miss Dynamite could handle herself well.

Exhausted from the trauma of worrying over her granddaughter, Nana went to bed within a half hour or so, leaving me alone with Lola. "My father was there, wasn't he?"

She pretended to zip her lips. I chortled and said she'd better fess up.

"I can't. I promised."

I could feel my eyes widen. "You've got to be kidding."

"No, I'm not." Again, she zipped her lips, while I fumed over her unwillingness to be open with me over my father's daring deed.

"Think it over, Lola. You might change your mind in a day or so."

The screen door creaked a tad and I jumped to my feet, the wine bottle held as a weapon in my hand. Steps drew near and Marcus entered the room. His expression serious, I quaked in my shoes.

"What is it?"

"Sit down, Vin. Relax."

"No, what's wrong?"

"Jimmy Byrne and Burgatti are dead. Aaron has a minor injury, but he'll be all right. He's been flown to the mainland. What do you know about this evening's events?"

Shocked at the news, my knees grew weak and I sagged onto the sofa. Aaron was all right. "Sit, and I'll tell you," I said softly as Lola gave me a look filled with shock of her own. She snuggled into her corner of the sofa.

He took the nearest armchair, crossed his legs, and waited patiently. I gave him a synopsis of what had happened to Lola, who had taken her, and why, and then ended up with a lie. "As Aaron and I were about to rescue Lola, a group of men arrived and saved the day. We left in a hurry, knowing she would be okay, and then came back here." I left out the fact that my father had been on hand, had acted on Lola's behalf, and that Quatrini was behind the scenes. I didn't consider these out and out lies, but lies by omission, which amount to the same thing. The important thing was protecting my father, and that would happen, no matter the cost.

His attention on me, he didn't notice Lola's relief when I omitted my father's part in the whole affair. We all have to be thankful for the little things, don't we?

" It seems that all has ended well for you and Lola. I take it you'll be leaving for the mainland soon?"

"Most likely in the morning. I can't wait to get home. I've had enough excitement to last me for some time. What happened with the mobsters last night?"

He gave me a long look and said, "Burgatti and Jimmy decided to have it out, which was something we expected. Aaron arrived as things were just getting started, and was struck by a stray bullet. He was lucky his injury wasn't worse. Jimmy shot Burgatti, and one of Burgatti's men killed Jimmy. The rest of the men surrendered to the police.

I opened my mouth to ask more about Aaron's condition, but was interrupted by Lola.

"You're sure Aaron will be all right? Really sure?" Lola asked.

Marcus nodded. "I am. And, I'm happy that you're back safe and sound."

He stood, put his campaign hat on since he was in uniform, and walked out.

I heard his motorcycle start and then he roared off down the road.

Lola blew out a hefty sigh. "For a second, I thought you were going to spill your guts to Marcus." She snickered. "I should have known better than that, shouldn't I?"

"Indeed. Now, I'm packing my bags and we're leaving this island, tomorrow morning. You must want to see Jack, and I should check on Aaron. Then I'll stop by my father's house, as he and I need to talk."

We headed upstairs, and though it was late, we both packed our bags. I didn't sleep well and was up with the sun. I sat on the dock, watched birds fly overhead, land on the inlet, and then take off again. I sipped hot coffee, considered life was good once again, and waited for Nana and Lola to begin their day.

Having eaten breakfast together, the three of us discussed the past few weeks happenings, and then Lola, Nana and I drove to the ferry landing. We waited to return home while Nana kept us company until the ferry was ready to leave. While we bought our ferry tickets, Dave Martin stopped by. He wished us well, asked us to never return, and then smiled to soften the insult.

Nana stepped up and said, "Dave Martin, you just hold on for one minute. Since my granddaughter and Vinnie have been on this island, you've done nothing but harass them and make a fool of yourself. I'll be having a word or two with your mother over your behavior. Mark my word on that."

We watched his discomfort at being told off by a little old grandmother, and for a mere second or so, I felt sorry for the man. It wasn't long before he gave us a nod and left.

I grinned. "He's not a happy man, but the racketeers are gone, some were arrested, and others, well, who knows if they're on ice somewhere waiting to be disposed of. All I know is, I can't wait for my life in Scituate to resume."

The trip to Galilee, the port where our ferry would land, was marvelous. We sat on the open deck, watched the gulls dip and dive, and talked of nothing important. Maybe Lola would tell me what I wanted to know about my father's part in her rescue, and maybe she wouldn't. Either way, it was her decision and I respected that.

We didn't go straight to Scituate after we disembarked from the ferry, but instead we drove straight to the hospital, and went to see Aaron and Jack. I called Rhode Island Hospital to check if Aaron was indeed there instead of one of the other hospitals in Providence. I was relieved that he'd been taken to the trauma unit, instead of being treated at the hospital on the island. They weren't set up for any real trauma, like Rhode Island Hospital was.

Happy to see us, both men promised to get well, but only if we continued to visit regularly. I told Lola to wait for me in the lobby, and took a seat next to Aaron's bed. She glanced at Aaron, said she'd see me shortly, and closed the door on her way out of the room.

"I'm really pleased to see you doing so well. What's going to happen to you now? Will you be able to return to active duty or have you blown your cover?"

With a sigh, a twinkle in his eyes, and laying his hand on mine, Aaron said, "Once I've been released, I'll have a round of physical therapy, and then it's back to work. Thankfully, I didn't blow my cover, things were well underway by the time I reached the yacht, and no one was the wiser. Besides, it's convenient that I was wounded, it set the stage for my return to the underworld." He squeezed my hand and said I could be his nurse if I so desired.

I laughed outright at his words, and dashed his hopes with a shake of my head. "I'll be back to see you again. You have my number, just call me. And, I'll pick you up when you've been released, okay? Would you like to tell me everything that occurred onboard the yacht?"

"Sorry, I can't. You knew that, anyway, so why ask? You just couldn't help yourself." He thanked me for coming by. I rode the elevator down to the lobby to meet Lola.

We drove to the western side of Little Rhody, where we could both sleep in our own beds.

After Lola dropped me off, I tossed my dirty laundry in the hamper and sat outside on the deck behind my house. The house phone rang. My father was on the line.

"Are you busy, Lavinia?"

"Not at the moment," I said coolly.

"I'll be coming by shortly."

I hung up and went back to sit on the deck. My mind traveled over what the upcoming conversation might entail and frankly, I wasn't up for an argument. I wanted peace and quiet, no mobsters, no trouble, nothing that would create havoc in my life, at least for a while.

Sometime later, a car door closed, and my father entered the hallway. I invited him in and peered behind him before I asked, "Where's Mom?"

He slid onto a seat at the kitchen counter. "She's off with your aunt Josephine. They went shopping."

"Oh. Can I make you an Espresso?"

"Not right now. I want to talk about what happened on the island."

"Frankly, Dad, I don't care to discuss it. Not now, not ever, if you don't mind."

Dad's stare never left my face. He didn't blink, flinch, or seem to breathe, though he must have for he was alive.

"I did what I thought best."

"You keep secrets from me. It's unacceptable."

"I have to."

Let me say this about my father, he's never, ever explained himself, he's never apologized, and definitely never looked for acceptance from anyone. What had happened to make him do so now? I had no clue.

My father drummed his fingertips on the countertop. "After Rudy was killed, I knew I had to interfere. It was a difficult decision to make, but necessary. That's all I can say."

"Fine, let's leave it at that." The questions were piling up fast, and if I wasn't careful, they'd spill out of my mouth like an overflowing riverbed. It was enough that Dad had owned up to stepping in, and that, I could accept. He'd done what he had to, and I'd willingly let him off the hook for it. After all, hadn't Quatrini said in so many words that what I didn't know couldn't be held against me?

I gave him a huge hug, said everything was all right, and sent him on his way. Right now, life was really good, and for that, I was grateful.

# J.M. Griffin Novels

## The Vinnie Esposito Series
For Love of Livvy
Dirty Trouble
Cold Moon Dead
Season For Murder
Death Gone awry
Deader Than Dead
? ?

## The Luna Devere Series
### Faerie Cake Dead
### Faerie Dust Dead

??

**The Sarah McDougall Series**
**Murder on Spyglass Lane**
**The Cadence Caper**

? ?

The Deadly Bread Series
A Crusty Murder
A Crouton Murder
The Focaccia Fatality

? ?

## The Bun & Jules Series
Left Fur Dead
Who's Dead Doc?
Hop 'Til You Drop
? ?

**Single Title Novels**
**Tangled To Death**
**The Man, The Dog & Murder**
**Dragon's Touch**

? ?

# A Romance Novella
# The Billionaire's Take

## ABOUT THE AUTHOR

J.M. Griffin is the author of seventeen published mystery novels, including the Jules & Bun cozy mysteries. As a member of Mystery Writers of America, Sisters in Crime National and Sisters in Crime New England, J.M. also holds membership in Novelist's Inc. A traditionally and independently published author, when she's not writing, J.M. can be found in her art studio accompanied by two very mysterious cats.